# THE WIND
# OF FATHERS

## A NOVEL

BUNIS W. WALKER

The Wind of Fathers

ISBN 978-0-615-32322-0

*For my grandmother Myrtle Ford Walker*

# Chapter One

KANE CONTINUED TO GRIMACE, turning on his back for a third time. He could not sleep. It was the fourth night this week that his stomach was left squirming from his mother's cooking.

He endured her unsavory meals all his life, over fifteen years and, although she tried, her well-fought dishes were usually left undevoured. He decided to dull the pain by musing over Shyla, an orderly schoolgirl who just entered his high school a few weeks ago.

A tall beauty she was—one that wore a rich cinnamon complexion complimenting her over-developed figure. She enjoyed a daily hoard of horny teens, all ready to carry her books and finish off her homework at her slightest whim. Each morning, Kane, blessed with her presence in English class, made certain his look was of the very best before leaving for school - an interesting challenge given his deteriorating wardrobe. Dimitri, one of Kane's better friends was kept amused by Kane's pitiful quest to one day capture the heartbreaking beauty. To him, she was unreachable—out of Kane's league. Nonetheless, Kane remained determined, especially given his embarrassing status. He was still a virgin, amongst a sea of teenagers having sex practically every day. A gloomy reality. He hoped God was not playing a cruel joke on him. To make things worst, two weeks ago, he nearly revealed his secret during health education class.

---

*"Okay, next week is the test. If you don't have last week's notes, please follow me to my office," said Mr. Albright, his health education teacher, in a loud tone. The over-the-top professor could always be counted on for overextending his voice.*

*"Mr. A," Kane muttered softly as they both headed for the front door. "When you said that everyone in the class will be sexually active, did you really mean everyone?" Kane could not believe he asked, but felt he had to. His hormones were raging out of control; he was more concerned with answers now.*

*"Yes, everyone in this class—including you—will be sexually active someday, so protect yourself and study for the test," Mr. Albright shouted at him, with much of the class standing directly behind.*

*Kane responded quickly, "Well, I'm already protecting myself!" His voice soared too high to be natural. If any of his classmates standing behind him had paid attention, they would have easily sensed the dishonesty in his voice. Luckily, for him, they were too busy poking fun at Benjamin's undersized pant—the only nerd in the class.*

*"Well, good, now just don't forget to study," Mr. Albright responded, as four students followed him down the hall.*

---

Suddenly, Kane's daydream was broken up by the sharp sound of his brother's oversized foot. Craig. His size thirteen's were always good for banging against the bedpost every now and then.

He tried to refocus on Shyla. He turned on his side to face the window and then pulled up the window shade quietly, ensuring his brother's sleep went undisturbed. He wanted to see the oversized oak tree just to the right of the window. If viewed at a certain angle on a clear night, the moonlight would pierce through the branches, creating a rather spooky scene; strangely Kane thought it was romantic.

Although the night sky was not clear, the silhouette of branches still managed to create a sanctuary for him. Relieved, he could now think of the love of his life in peace. He collected his pillow and started in on his never-ending fantasies.

Shyla and Kane, a couple. They spoke once, something he thought of constantly, a thought that proved to always be a good segue into his overextended delusions. Her books had slipped from her grasp and landed just a few feet from him. Collecting them quickly, he simply muttered, "I got it, Shyla."

She turned towards him with a natural smile, mixed with both confusion and sincerity. He said her name with a familiar tone, as if they had known each other for years.

"Oh, thanks," she replied in a soft voice. That was the whole of the engagement – almost embarrassing to keep hold of such a thing.

The quiet of the room made his eyes heavy. It was time for yet another one of his dreams.

—

*The door creaked open slightly as tiny footsteps brushed against Aunt Mable's dusty wooden floor. It was Kane's rowdy cousin Robert. He entered the room slowly, with a white towel carefully wrapped around his eyes.*

*Kane always dreaded the idea of playing Blind Man Bluff in a house this big, although today would not be the typical game. Shyla was there. Her presence was sure to invite a more stirring mood, at least for Kane.*

*He took her by the hand and slid beneath Aunt Mable's sleigh-style day bed in the guest room. The tiny room was trivial though, it had two exits, making it a smart place to hide.*

*Blind Man Bluff,* one of Kane's favorite childhood games, was always the first choice for amusement when there was a lack of adult supervision. A game that left one unlucky soul blindfolded in search of a band of scattered kids. Robert was the unlucky one for the moment, though his extra gusto usually made his tour short-lived.

"Should we move?" Shyla whispered as soft as she could, after she heard Robert's footsteps nearing the bed. Suddenly, the sound of fallen toiletries came from the guest bathroom next to the doorway. It prompted Robert's exit into the other room.

At last, Kane had Shyla to himself. Taking full advantage, he positioned his body against hers and although they became fused together, the arrangement was a bit awkward to invite any meaningful foreplay. In addition, privacy was still an issue. Light from the sun made its' way beneath the bed. It kept their secret uncovered for the moment.

*I just need to pull the comforter down a bit,* Kane plotted to himself.

With one jerk, he tugged the rose-colored comforter off the neatly made mattress and the last specs of light fell into complete darkness. He could not see a thing, only the shadows cast by her white tank top. She turned quickly and faced him, then planted a healthy kiss across his lips. He welcomed it, of course, but considered the limited amount of time for anything meaningful.

In a failed attempt to position himself on top of her, he fell back annoyed with the small amount of space beneath the bed. He remained fixed on his side as Shyla waited still for his next move. Desperately he wanted her to turn on her side, in a spooning position, but felt it would have been too bold to suggest it.

With time running thin, his impatience worked up the nerve to reach out and unfasten her belt. His eyes lifted – surprised, as his anxious fingers found her belt already undone. The bulge from his Levis came to an *embarrassing swell. He took notice of her opened zipper and hesitated no longer. Being careful became a swallowed thought.*

*He pulled his grey colored chinos down to his ankles, exposing his underwear. She followed behind swiftly, removing her jeans, leaving behind her childish pink and white panties for the showing. She smiled nervously.*

*Suddenly, Kane slammed his head against the bedpost, startled. Someone had barged through the side door. He quickly grabbed Shyla towards him attempting to shield himself from the embarrassment. In her own panic, she turned around in an effort to pull up her jeans. Unbeknownst to her, she inadvertently landed in the position that he had been struggling with for the past few minutes. He quickly grabbed her hand and stopped her from pulling up her jeans.*

*As the grey and white Adidas hovered beneath the comforter, Kane knew it was Damen, his other cousin. He slammed the door against the wall while running through the room. He suspected Robert was close by, but he was not about to move from his newly found position. Shyla's back was pressed firmly against his chest. With her jeans still down he was able to feel her curvy ass pressed against his briefs. It had been the closest he'd come to having sex.*

*Damen had long passed, though Shyla remained fixed in the same position. Sunlight trickled in beneath the bed. Damen managed to create a slight gap from his careless bump that shifted the comforter slightly. Shyla. He could see her now—the side of her smooth face and rich, brown skin. Her head, turned towards the floor, her arms locked at her sides; she clutched her fist and braced for pain. He paused, and then peaceful undressed the rest of her.*

*Moments later, he realized he was nearly inside of her, stopped only by the thin cotton of his briefs. The sensation was intoxicating – enthralling, even against the impeding underwear. Softly, he shifted over ever so slightly to remove the last obstruction.*

*The air became still.*

*Quiet.*

*The room now had a light coolness, which made his heart stop racing. And the sweat that once poured from his forehead started to dissipate. He managed to sigh privately, relieved that he was finally going to make love to Shyla—the love of his life.*

*He pulled at his briefs but found he could not remove them. Were they stuck against something? A nail from the floor perhaps? He tugged harder, still no luck. Again he pulled, but still nothing. Before long, he entered into a wild struggle, tearing at his underwear—extracting the romance from the mood.*

*In the midst of his tussle, the mattress was thrown clear from the day-bed, exposing the both of them. It was Robert. His small fingers were fastened tightly around Kane's left ankle. He pulled at Kane's leg and shouted, "You're it! You're it!" Both enraged and embarrassed, Kane angrily kicked at Robert's right arm; a cruel attempt to release the unusual stiff grasp on his leg. It did not work.*

*How could he be this strong? Kane pondered. Robert continued his violent heave. Seconds later, the little pest geared up to deliver a healthy strike. He wouldn't dare, Kane thought.*

*Kane's eyes went red after a loud pummel crossed his left calf. Robert had struck him, but before Kane could strike back, he realized the person that stuck him was not Robert but his brother, Craig. An awful reality began to unfold as he watched in anguish. Shyla's face. It had faded into blackness. His dream had ended.*

---

"Shit, I was dreaming!" Thwarted, Kane shook his head in deep disappointment, as he listened to Craig shout, "Kane, wake up! Wake up!" Frustrated and angered by the dream, Kane was all ready to take issue with Craig over the intrusion, but found their small apartment was already in chaos.

It was their father again. The doctors said the man should have been dead already. Years of drinking damaged his liver. Moreover, his unyielding appetite for Newport 100's, left him short of breath and worn out most of the time. Everyone in the apartment complained about getting lung cancer because of the constant smoke. Most times, Kane cleverly avoided his father's bouts of severe choking, which usually brought their small apartment into complete hysteria. His aunt's apartment in Coney Island was the safe zone. Unfortunately, he was present for this one, which seemed to be more serious than the others.

*What happened to us?* Kane thought as he jumped down from the bunk bed. He stood there frozen in thought, reluctant to move another inch.

"Kane, dad is on the floor! Come on! Shit!" Craig shouted at him as if Kane carried a medical license. After his sister, Jade, left everyone in the house cursed, except for Kane's mother. They had also stopped attending their church, the Kingdom Hall, which added to their declining behavior. Now, they were teenagers in a deep struggle to finish high school, and with their mother too strained to put up a meaningful fight, dropping out seemed more likely for the both of them. Far from the good old days.

"What happened?" Kane asked, still recovering from one of his better dreams of Shyla.

"He's choking again," Craig replied sharply, and then raced back into the bedroom.

Kane overheard his Uncle Bo's voice in the other room. There was no doubt in his mind that his father was drinking and getting high with him. Finally, he made his way out of his room, but found two strangers who reeked of alcohol was there to greet him. The stench was so strong he had to cover his nose as he passed them by—clearly some of Uncle Bo's friends.

"Hey, little man," said one of them, as he tried to fix himself straight. Kane ignored the lengthy man and entered into his father's bedroom.

It took a moment for him to register the scene in front of him: his father was lying on the floor next to the nightstand with Uncle Bo hovered over him jamming a spoon into his mouth. Instantly, Kane recognized what was wrong. His father was having a seizure—another one.

"I'm trying to…" said Uncle Bo. He struggled to steady the cheap piece of silverware lodged at the base of Kane father's mouth. His mother could not bare the sight of it. She had her face planted against the bedroom window, waiting anxiously for the ambulance. Kane remained fixed in the doorway, but kept his head turned away. Wisely, he spared himself the sight, but between his father's violent gags and Uncle Bo's hysterical grunts his fists clutched in nervousness. The noises grew louder and his uncle's muttering became more desperate. His dad was known for escaping these episodes, but this one seemed different.

"Shit, Gary, hold still," Uncle Bo pleaded.

Suddenly, the gagging stopped. Kane found the courage to take a quick peek. The room fell still. He stole a glance and saw part of his father's arm violently twitching. He looked desperate, clinging on to life.

*Could it be?*

*Could he really die here…now?*

*My dad.*

Kane thought back to a memorable day in the summer of 1977.

"I got ya," said his father in a relaxed tone. "I won't let go, okay?" His voice continued to soften, as he tried to hold back a smirk.

Kane was six years old, learning to swim at Betsy Head, a local pool two blocks from their apartment. His father patiently helped him along. His little fist wrapped the metal rail for dear life while his father gently tugged at his waist. The water was colder than usual and to worsen the moment, he was forced to listen to heckles from his older brother. "Pull him in, dad pull him!" Craig shouted as Kane gripped the rail even tighter.

Tiny, but fierce, he turned to stare down at the bearded man and saw only his gentle smile and strong grip around his waist. Finally, Kane's small fingers decided to release its hold. His father's face was teeming with love. Kane had only his father's word that his trusting hands would remain fastened around his waist.

"Kick, stupid," Craig yelled with a wide smile.

"Kanie, kick...slowly," his father suggested. Within seconds, Kane calmed himself and began his trek, leaving behind a modest path of fresh waves. His father's hands still fastened around his side.

He loved his father then. The man was happy and quietly smiled at nearly everything.

———

Uncle Bo's sudden outburst pulled Kane from his thoughts.

"Damn it!" Uncle Bo yelled in frustration with Kane's father now lying motionless on the bedroom floor. In a panic, Bo began ripping off his brother-in-law's t-shirt, preparing for CPR. His mother trembled, uncontrollably. She flopped on the bed, drained. Unable to endure anymore, Kane dashed into his sister's old room and slammed the door shut. He sat in a corner, and let his emotions take over as his heart began to pound through his chest. He just wanted the commotion to end. No such luck.

A loud bang came from the front door.

Then again.

The force of the knock caused pieces of old paint chips to fall from the hinges. The loud bangs reminded Kane of the time the police came looking for Darryl, his brother's friend. It was a deafening noise.

"They're here, Mom! They're here," Craig shouted, as he took flight for the front door; hoping for EMT workers.

The front door swung open.

"Where's the patient?" asked the police officer sharply.

"My dad is in the bedroom," said Craig, wiping the tears from his eyes. A pile of men rushed in after the officer. It seemed like the police had invited the entire hospital along.

Although Kane had quietly parked himself in his sister's old room and covered his ears, he still could not escape the sounds of keys jangling, walkie-talkies blasting, and medical equipment slamming against the metal closet.

"Please step aside, sir," instructed the medic, clearly unhappy about the stench of malt liquor beneath Uncle Bo's breath. Uncle Bo tried to explain the situation to the police officer as he departed from the bedroom. "I think he had a stroke. I was trying to..." cutting Uncle Bo off, the agitated officer again asked him to step aside.

The head medic ordered everyone out of the room. Abruptly, he shut the bedroom door so they could work on the unlucky soul.

The crowded apartment was left to listen to the beeping sounds from a portable respirator and the constant shuffling of medical tools being pulled from duffle bags. Even Uncle Bo's drunk friends remained quiet. Everyone tuned in to the chilling racket of the respirator. Still tucked away in Jade's old room, Kane suddenly thought of his mother. *She's out there alone. I should be with her.* He immediately stood up and took a deep breath to calm his nerves. Turning the light to his sister's room back on, Kane opened the door slowly and headed back towards the spectacle.

To Kane's surprise, his brother was holding their mother by the waist, with Uncle Bo clenching four of her fingers in comfort.

"Come here, Kane," his mother cried out, sounding as if the man was already dead. Kane fell towards her chest in complete frailty.

*Why does he put us through this?* Kane wondered. His mother and brother surely did not deserve this torment—no one did.

Kane's hug tightened around his mother's waist. The beeping sound went softer, heightening their fears. Uncle Bo's friend, DJ, left and headed towards Kane's room—most likely to light a smoke out of the window.

"Okay, let's go," shouted the medic in an urgent voice as the bedroom door flew open. They all made room as the medics headed for the front door.

Kane stared down at his father, who was firmly strapped to an orange stretcher with huge metal clamps fastened across his face. The stretcher left behind a smell of rubbing alcohol and sterilized equipment. It smelled like the hospital. It smelled like death.

"Only one can come in the ambulance," the male medic instructed. There was no question Kane's mother was going. She headed straight for the closet and grabbed her coat before anyone else had a thought.

Kane felt relieved for the moment, perhaps his father would have a second chance at life. Then a quick jolt of reality made him realize how likely it was that this ordeal would reoccur. The truth was simple; his father was battling more than seizures. He was battling an addiction. The only cure for addicts is the desire to rehabilitate and it seemed the man trashed that idea years ago.

Kane glared at the nearly unrecognizable man on the stretcher, and battled his spiraling emotions. Although frustrated by his father's carelessness for his life, Kane could not help but feel a strong sense of love for the man. He knew that, despite all of his father's faults, his love for him out-stretched everything as he managed to touch the back end of the stretcher.

Five seconds after the front door had closed, Uncle Bo and his friends left the apartment, claiming that they needed to see someone across town. Kane would have bet everything he had that they were headed to Rauhal's Liquor Store for another drink.

*Deadbeats.*

"I'm moving," Craig said, shaking his head as he stared down at the crowd from the living room window. They looked on as the ambulance carried their father away.

"I'm going to stay with Keisha. Her mother said I could sleep in the living room." Keisha was Craig's girlfriend of three years.

Kane was not surprised, as his brother continued to detail his plan. He was upset to hear the news, but was more agitated about everything else—his father, school—his life. Despite feeling slightly abandoned, Kane was actually happy that his brother had the opportunity to leave; especially given his ongoing problems with Big Ant, a guy who accused Craig of flirting with his girlfriend. Big Ant was a known killer with a huge following. Leaving Brooklyn completely was a smart move.

Just then, Kane heard a knock at the front door.

Looking through the peephole, he saw the familiar black, hooded-sweatshirt leaning against the side of the wall. It was Dimitri.

Kane opened the front door.

"You alright?" asked Dimitri, concerned for Kane, as he let himself in. Kane nodded yes and headed for his room.

Dimitri had been with Kane through a few of these attacks before. He knew to keep quiet. He followed Kane into the back room giving Craig a head nod. "What's up?"

Moments later.

"Craig, I'm going to the store…want something?" Kane asked. He hoped his brother would say no. All he had left in his pocket was five dollars that he won in a dice game last week.

"Yeah, a forty…St. Ides," Craig shouted, still looking down from the living room window.

Damn, why didn't he say some potato chips or something? Kane mumbled.

The front door closed behind them as they headed off to the store.

Although they were nearly the same age, Dimitri was always the one elected to buy beer from the store. He looked a little older although, it really did not matter most times. If you were old enough to carry beer, the corner stores would let you buy it.

Craig occasionally smoked weed, but after the night's spectacle, his request did not come as a surprise. Although some of his friends would indulge in 40-ounce bottles of malt liquor, Kane never partook. Aside from despising the awful aftertaste, as he watched his family members enjoying bottle after bottle, he noticed that it seemed to do more damage than good.

Meanwhile, at the hospital.

Hours felt like days. Kane's mother, worn out and anxious, sat alone. Four hours had passed. She had already called her sister, Dorothy six times. The night had exhausted her. There was nothing to do but think about her ailing husband.

"Mrs. Davis," said the nurse as she escorted her out of the waiting area, into a small conference room down the hall, "The doctor will be with you shortly." The nurse remained unemotional and refused to surrender any news, despite his mother's frequent questions. The only response the nurse gave was the rehearsed, "The doctor will be with you shortly, ma'am, sorry."

Another thirty minutes had passed. She stood by the window, staring down at a few cars that flew pass on the empty expressway. Just then, the door opened behind her. Her heart dropped to the floor as she slowly turned around.

Dr. Van Dalion entered the room, worn out, sweat still trickling down his face. "Mrs. Davis…we lost him." The doctor wasted no time. No matter how often he delivered this type of news, it never got easier.

"I'm so sorry," the doctor said in a quiet voice.

She collapsed into his arms—tearless, mouth open wide—shouting in a mute pain. The look of failure stretched cross his washed-out face. He was no stranger to death, but he had not lost a patient since he transferred from California Medical back in 1986. He placed her down softly in the chair and watched as the tears rolled down her face. Her arms wobbled lifelessly as she buried her head on the conference table. Two nurses raced over for comfort. No one said a word for nearly two minutes; they all patiently waited for the doctor's cue.

Finally, after another two long minutes, the doctor ordered the nurses to stay with her for a while. He exited the conference room slowly, with his head lowered in disappointment.

An hour had passed; it was nearly 5:00am. The nurses called her sister Dorothy to pick her up.

Forty minutes later.

"Oh, Karen," said Dorothy, arriving in tears with her husband. "Let's go home." Dorothy felt both the physical and emotional weight of her sister as she helped her off the chair.

In a weak voice, Kane's mother mumbled, "I can't go to that place tonight. I can't…I just can't."

They collected her things and took a cab back to Dorothy's apartment.

The next morning.

The apartment reeked of alcohol and cigarettes. Craig's friend Darryl also came by, along with a few others. They were awake nearly the entire night listening to Kane and Craig rap to the instrumental side of The Youngsters album, an up-and-coming rap group. It was a crazy night, but it felt well-deserved after their father's violent collapse.

Kane found himself back on the floor in his sister's room, tucked away in the corner. He wanted to be as far away from his father's bedroom as possible.

The phone rang, breaking the silence that had spread though the apartment. It rang sixteen times before Craig finally decided to knock it over with the back of his hand.

"Yeah?" Craig mumbled into the phone, barely conscious.

"Craig?" The familiar voice on the other end belonged to Jade, who had received the news first.

"Yeah." Craig was still trying to shake off last night's liquor.

Almost like vomit, the foul words just spilled from her mouth. "He died." Her voice cracked in agony.

Craig held a long pause that felt like days. Jade's two words began to sink in as his face started to swell with tears.

He thought of his brother. With their father now gone, Jade's rare visits to house, and his own plans to leave within a few days, he wondered how Kane would manage.

# Chapter Two

SIX MONTHS HAD PASSED since the death of Kane's father. His brother only visited twice after the funeral and, on both occasions, it was just to drop off a few bucks for their mother. Craig had started working at a supermarket in New Jersey a few months ago and was still living with Keisha.

Kane missed his big brother, but he was happy that he was away, safe from Big Ant. The last time Craig has visited, he mentioned that he was getting his GED. After dropping out of school six months ago, it was good news. He seemed to have developed a new focus in his life.

As for Kane, his grades were slipping. If it was not for Tileyah and Dimitri, he would have dropped out of school altogether by now.

Eventually, his mother returned to the apartment, but she stayed in Jade's old room. His parent's bedroom became the new storage room for Jade and Craig's uncollected things. For a while, it was hard to walk pass the creepy room without tighten up with emotion. The mere site of the closed door kept him reminded of that dreadful day.

A few weeks after the funeral, his mother began to fall ill. She stopped eating regularly and developed blistering migraines. Too fragile to worry about Kane, she kept herself in the room for much of the time. He welcomed her absence and would test her patience constantly.

It was May and the weather was changing. The leaves nearly filled the branches—Kane's seventeenth birthday was a week away. He was not expecting anything from anyone, just maybe a call from his sister.

He was going to be a seventeen-year-old virgin. This was the only thing that filled his thoughts. He just wanted to find a way to get some nice clothes. Catching Shyla's eye was an ongoing mission, one that he was determined to accomplish. He was still interested, even after he found her lips wrapped around Sterling's mouth, on the side of the stairwell a few months ago. Sterling was a bit of a jock from the basketball team – a guy with more girls than he needed. Shyla was to him, just another girl to swell his already inflated ego.

Kane, on the other hand, was in a deep obsession. Through all of his countless dreams, he felt like he knew her, even though he did not speak with her much in class. Nearly an entire school year went by, and he could count the number of times he got up the courage to throw some words her way. Also, looking nice on a daily basis for Shyla was a serious challenge. After his father's death their welfare check had shrunk and money was even tighter. Kane took his allowance and gambled it away. It was a desperate attempt to add to a very humbling amount of pocket money; an amount so thin it kept him struggling to afford even the cheapest pair of jeans.

It was his never ending dice games that gave him hope. Kane's obsession with playing dice was something Dimitri could never understand, especially when he gambled around 654 near Myrtle Street. He felt the building was crazy and did not trust the strange crowds of people that hung out over there. Dimitri would never go with him. He was stuck most times taking Tileyah, the biggest tomboy on the block, though after losing the glasses a few years ago, she did not look half-bad. Rumor had it she still liked him, but he was too interested in getting money for clothes to care.

With his birthday coming up next Friday, he intended to look his very best. He also picked that day to make a move on Shyla. He was going to ask her out for lunch to Aaron's Jamaican Bakery on the corner near the school. Kids at school ate there every day, but Kane could not afford that kind of luxury, at least not on a daily basis. He was stuck with the food from the cafeteria most of the time.

Pacing around his room, he decided to take his last fifteen dollars to a dice game at 654. He didn't like the building any more than Dimitri did, especially since the front lights were always out, darkening an already gloomy area. But, his friend Daren lived over there giving him just enough comfort to kill his fears. Daren. It was never a good dice game without his humorous taunting.

Kane opened the front door to the apartment building and made his way off the front stoop. *Who can I get to come with me?* He surveyed the front of the building.

Everyone was outside, except for Dimitri.

Stefan, the bully of the block was out; Kane couldn't stand the site of him. His father had died of an overdose two years ago. His mother too, was no stranger to drugs. A dirty rumor once circled the block that his mother tried to sell sex to Kane's uncle, Bo. It was just the ammunition Stef needed to hassle Kane. He did it every chance he could.

He caught Lionel's eye, but he was not a good option. The short-stubby guy was known for running at the first sign of trouble – not the type of person you want guarding your back. Tileyah was the safe choice, but the last thing Kane wanted was this already nosey block to think they were a couple.

"Yo, Kane. What up?" Stef was leaning on the tree as he watched over the Skelly game.

"You seen Dee?" Kane asked. He planned to beg Dimitri to tag along, just this once. He certainly wasn't going to ask Stef.

*How could Stef be so stupid and not see how many people didn't like him?* Kane wondered as he continued his search.

"Nah, I think he's upstairs, why? What's up?" Stef answered, turning back to the game.

Kane didn't bother to answer him.

*I had better decide while it's still light out,* he thought anxiously. Just then, he noticed the trusty Tileyah. He almost did not recognize her in that striped colored blouse; it was a bit girly for her.

"Tileyah, come with me to 654?" Kane asked with an exaggerated smile. Kneeling, she slowly turned her head up towards him and sighed. "Can't, I'm waiting to go to the movies with my mother."

*That would explain her hairdo and the nice-looking clothes.* He did not want to beg, but had no choice. Good dice games are hard to find and according to Daren this one would have some decent players with money.

"Okay, just walk me over there then. I just want to see if they're playing." Kane asked as he pulled at the sleeve on her blouse. After she looked up at his smile, she agreed. The 654 apartment building was only ten minutes away, but it seemed like a foreign country in many ways. If you didn't live in the building, you could not escape the icy glares handed out when you stepped around the block.

They approached the block. Sure enough, a full-blown dice game was in progress with all the normal players including his trusty companion, Daren. As usual, he was acting a fool—ensuring his voice was lifted above everyone else's.

"Please, stay for one game?" Kane begged, pulling Tileyah along by her wrist. He put on a charming smile again. She gave him a frustrated look but continued behind him.

Daren welcomed him into the mix "Yo, Kay! You in?"

Kane nodded "Yes," and slowly walked over. Dice was his game. Craig had taught him everything, even though much of it was luck.

He knew a few of the guys standing around, but the rest were strangers. Going down on one knee, he carefully placed himself a few feet from the other players. He did not want to agitate anyone. Half of the beefs in the projects came from playing dice. He knew it was dangerous, but he'd never had a bad experience playing on this block. There was the usual light-hearted bitching, but nothing too serious. Besides, the most he had ever won in one night was around twenty-five dollars, never enough to create a real stir. However, tonight he wanted to win big, at least a hundred bucks, a bit ambitious, but do-able.

Two hours passed.

The block went black with Tileyah still by his side. The front overhead lights automatically shut off at 9:00 pm. It left the block darker than normal. The game continued on, all players tense. Kane was up sixty dollars. Daren, now drunk had gotten more animated by the minute. He drew the strange crowd Dimitri always spoke of. You couldn't tell if the person next to you was a murderer or an A student. The game was surrounded. Kane was on a roll. Of course, his streak did not go without protest. One player had lost thirty bucks. He insisted that Kane was cheating.

*How could I cheat at this game?* Kane pondered. *What an idiot.* He knew Kane did not bring the dice. Naturally, he was just upset about his losses. Kane did not care. Locked in, he needed only another forty bucks. Some of the more familiar people in the crowd cheered him on.

Noticeably frustrated by the time, Tileyah still managed to keep herself next to him. *Maybe she does like me,* Kane thought, looking up catching her eye. *Oh well, she missed her movie and she most likely would be punished for staying off the block so long.*

Kane could not think pass the game; it was the most money he'd ever won. *Okay, another twenty minutes, then I'm out.* He briefly sympathized with Tileyah's situation but then turned his attention back to the game.

It was Kane's turn to roll. "A seven!" He shouted at the top of his lungs. The lucky roll brought him an extra fifteen dollars.

Everyone paid up, except for the same disgruntled player.

"I'm not giving you shit," the guy said, kicking the dice against the fence. Kane's heart dropped to his stomach. The sensation spiraled around his belly. The fuming player stood up, incensed. He waited impatiently for Kane's next response.

Kane was all ready to run, but knew if he did, he could never play dice around there again. Not to mention Daren; he would be sure to tell the whole school what happened. Kane had to fight now, or his already fragile reputation of being a bit of a hard rock, would come in question.

The last fight Kane had was with his brother, two weeks before his father passed away. Trying desperately to cover his fear, he stood up and prepared his fist into a fighting stance. The strange crowd and dark block softened him. He stood there gingerly with his fist barely protecting his face.

"What? You wanna fi—?" the guy pounced on Kane before he could finish his words. Their bodies crashed into the fence with Kane's back absorbing much of the blow.

It was now a race for position, as they rolled onto the stiff cement. Whoever got on top would be able to land clean blows to the face and body. Although still filled with nerves, Kane managed to gather some modest strength. He knew that if the guy managed to pin him down, he was a goner.

A sudden outburst came from the crowd. It was Tileyah.

"Get him, Kane! Get him," she continued as Kane grabbed the boy's shirt with conviction. He could not help but notice his strength over the disgruntled loud mouth. Despite his edgy state, Kane was clearly stronger. His nervousness faded sharply. He turned the boy's entire body over in one motion and pinned his back against the ground.

"Oh shit!" another voice shouted from the crowd. Kane placed his knee firmly against the boy's abs and was all ready to let off a few hooks to the face.

"You got it! You got it!" the defeated player said softly, hoping Kane was the one with ears for those words. In the projects, it was not clear what was worse: running from a fight or pleading during one. Either way, the guy was completely embarrassed.

Kane asked him several times if he was going to be cool after he released him. Held down hopelessly, the overpowered, sore loser replied, "Alright."

Kane decided to let him up. The loser suddenly jumped up, pouting. "Stay right there, motherfucker!" he yelled and headed for the building.

"He's going to get that broken gun. Such a punk!" A girl yelled out from the crowd.

*A gun!* Kane nearly blurted out the words aloud. He jumped up quickly to find Tileyah. She was just two feet behind him. He was impressed. Her brother, Lionel, would have been halfway down the block by now. Grabbing her hand, he slowly headed away from the block, which somehow seemed darker. The normally dim, overhead lights dangling from the cement canopy in front of the building had blown out. It was nearly pitch black, anyone could have taken a shot at him, and would have escaped unnoticed. It was a scary thought. *Time to leave.*

"Yo, Kay! Don't leave!" Daren said, laughing as if nothing happened. He looked on as Kane continued to make his way off the block. Kane did not want to seem like a punk, dashing off the block, so he decided to walk a bit slower than normal; but his nerves were certainly telling him to run.

They headed around the back of the building. Kane wasn't sure how serious this guy was. There were people who had been shot for much less around these parts.

As they turned off the block, Kane urged Tileyah to begin jogging. She did. Then a loud bang sounded off a short distance away. It was a gunshot. They stopped and looked at each other in disbelief. He released her hand, and they both sprinted for dear life.

After sprinting for ten minutes.

They stopped near the monkey bars in the back of 345, trying to catch their breath. Kane looked around frantically. He wanted to get out of the well-lit area so they headed for the noticeable black void about hundred yards away. It was Bryant Park. The night-lights were shut off. The out-dated park could not be creepier. It stood behind P.S. 231, an abandoned public school in the heart of the projects. It was a good place to hide.

Without looking back, they entered the park at full speed. They stopped behind a few old wooden benches which made for the perfect hiding place.

Crouched down between the bench and a high metal fence, they peeked and looked in all directions.

*Nothing.*

It seemed safe for the moment.

Kane relaxed his arm from the top of the bench to kneel down with Tileyah. She positioned herself a bit closer to him than normal.

She inched closer.

He felt her breasts across his back. Instantly, he became aroused and was determined not to budge from his spot. He asked her if she had seen anyone. "No," she replied, and then gently pressed closer.

The park was dark, empty and, with the moonlight glaring down on them, it reminded him of one of his dreams of Shyla.

"Wait," he said, "I think I just saw someone," he added, startled by some noisy ruffling from the other side of the park. It was most likely a rat. The park was known to be filled with them.

She wrapped her arms around his waist and pressed her breasts tightly against his back. Her breasts, they were the perfect size, and a deep smell of roses hidden beneath her pink stripped blouse turned him on even more. He turned towards her, looking over for a kiss. It seemed rather sudden, but their bodies were already speaking their own words.

He gently placed his hands around her waist, moving towards her face for a kiss. His heart began to race. Kane had not kissed a girl since Big Eric's block party last summer; Dimitri's older cousin, Tasha.

He moved closer.

She shivered.

Their mouths came together. Kane's deep plunge left their tongues to twist in heat. Her overly soft lips surprised him. Tileyah was a known tomboy, though tonight she was nothing of the sort.

He moved his hand towards her breasts. She paused sharply, pushing him back. Anxious, with lips swollen red from his kiss, her eyes said it all—unsure, confused, though still wanting him. She dropped back slowly, pulling him in closer.

Quickly, he glanced around and headed for the ground with her. With confidence, he lifted her blouse slightly over her bra. Her breasts were partially exposed. Her eyes remained fixed on his face.

He glazed over her chest and found her nipples protruding through her bra. It took all of two seconds for him to pull off her bra and wrap his lips around one of them. It was his very first time kissing breasts, but he continued like a pro. *It's about time*, he muttered silently to himself.

Suddenly, the fence made another shuttering sound off in a distance. He quickly jumped up to investigate as she pulled her blouse down.

Nothing again.

"It's nothing," Kane said, dropping back towards her. Anyone could have walked in the park, but they both continued anyway. They were dripping in heat, and for the first time, it wasn't one of his wild dreams of him and Shyla.

He went to kiss her again and then positioned himself between her legs, settling right on top of her. Firmly, he pressed against her jeans and began rubbing. He dropped his head towards her cheek, giving his full attention to the motion. She wrapped her arms around his waist, as his stroke developed a steady rhythm. Forgetting about the world, they both absorbed the vibrations of the moment.

A few minutes passed.

She slowly pushed him up, stopping in mid stride. His eyes followed her right hand as it went to unfasten her jeans. A slight tingle rushed through his chest as he paused in confusion. He did not know what to make of it.

*Are we going to have real sex,* he wondered; still puzzled.

Slowly, he helped her out of her blue denims. *Could it be? My first.* Kane's thoughts raced.

Within seconds her Levis were fully removed. He glanced over at a modest wet spot that came through her white panties. Nervously grinning, he unfastened his pants, praying it was not another dream.

After taking a deep breath, she pulled him next to her and whispered softly, "Please don't get me pregnant." His heart dropped. He turned his head in an attempt to conceal his nervousness.

It was happening.

Finally, his moment had arrived.

After a momentary pause, he softly peeled off her white panties, carefully aligned himself, and began a slow penetration.

The feeling was mystical, warm and cool at the same time. It was breathtaking. It was the missing piece to himself. The one he had always been seeking. *But, he had no idea it was like this.*

*Go slow, Kane,* he directed himself silently. He penetrated once more, slower this time. A small rhythm started. She moaned from the pain. A small tear dropped off the side of her face. She gazed over his face with worship. She loved him.

His eyes were closed shut. He thought of nothing—Shyla or anyone else. He tried to savor the moment of each stroke.

Three minutes later.

Leaning back against the fence, breathless, he thought of only leaving now. He had climaxed, and Tileyah's emotions were spiraling. She sat there and studied his every move.

They were still tucked away behind the wooden bench, absorbed in the smell of sex and sweat, but she could sense a slight withdrawal.

"Ready?" Kane nodded. He grabbed her hand and helped her off the pavement. It had been his first time, in a park no less. He was relieved, but couldn't help feeling as if a trusting innocence that he once possessed was now lost forever. This girl had taken his virginity. He finally thought of Shyla, his secret sweetheart. Feeling guilty, he slightly relaxed the grip on Tileyah's hand as they continued walking toward the block.

"Let's race," Kane said, pulling completely away from her—getting into a running position. Tileyah ran track for their high school. "Come on, you can't beat me," he said, hoping she'd agree to his bizarre challenge.

He wasn't ready for the block to know of their new-found love. He hoped to use the foot race as a way to release her hand and get some distance between them. It was surely the opposite for her; Tileyah was wearing an unmanageable glow across her face. *If only she knew.*

After passing him a strange look, she fell into position. There was no way in hell that he was going to win, and he knew it. He stopped playing basketball regularly ever since his father died. He was wondering if he would even make it around the block without stopping.

"Go!" Kane shouted, taking off in an honest attempt to win. Sure enough, she went blazing pass him in seconds, but his juvenile plan had worked.

The block was nearly empty though, only Stef and some other dude were outside sitting on the bench.

After listening to Stef carry on for a few minutes about how Tileyah was in trouble, they both went upstairs, drained from the excitement.

The next day, Kane didn't see her in front of the building. Her punishment was real. He didn't bother to come outside. Sundays were usually quiet anyway.

*Stef finally told the truth about something*, Kane thought as he moved away from the living room window. He felt bad that she was on punishment, but got the feeling that she did not care. The night was worth it. He liked Tileyah. But, as a girlfriend? He had never seen her that way. He passed the day in bed, thinking about everything. He needed a new place to play dice, and of course, he couldn't stop thinking about the night before.

However, despite what had happened between them, he still wanted to ask Shyla out. Each time he thought of her, an awkward sense of guilt clouded the moment. He'd wanted Shyla to be his first.

# Chapter Three

WITH SEVENTY DOLLARS in his pocket, he had enough to shop on Pitkin Avenue for a new pair of sneakers and a shirt.

"What size do you need?" The sales man asked, barely attentive as a shapely woman crossed between them.

"Twelve," Kane said, handing him a beige-colored Guess boot to reclaim his attention. The new Guess spring boots were a good choice. Everyone who had some money was jumping at the chance to buy them. Kane sought out the light beige; they'd go perfectly with his dark blue Levis jeans.

It was Thursday—his birthday was tomorrow. It was almost the end of a very strange week. Shyla had been absent from school for the past three days, sick perhaps or cutting class. He feared the worst for tomorrow.

*Would she show up?*

The week had exhausted him. Tileyah's never-ending harassment— stopping him in the hall every chance she could, had irritated him four days straight. Not to mention, Daren from 654 had been constantly reminding him of that disgruntle dice player from last Saturday—

claiming that the pest was planning to come up to the school and shoot him. Daren kept insisting that Kane leave last period early, maybe out the back of the school building. He went out the back on Monday, but the rest of the week, it was business as usual. For some reason, the guy didn't scare him anymore.

Kane was more worried about Tileyah's never-ending interrogations, and Shyla being absent from school for three days straight. Oddly enough, he felt Shyla had some sort of obligation to be there for him. He'd only spoken with her six times the entire school year, and it was likely she did not know him by name, yet he still felt a connection between them. Thank goodness, his outrageous infatuation was his little secret. Even Dimitri did not truly know how fixated Kane really was.

He hated shopping, especially on Pitkin Avenue, you'd always find a group of thugs staring down shopping bags, plotting to snatch them and take off running. He took the long way home after leaving the store; anything to avoid the troublemakers from the white houses—a shady project building off Maple Street.

Arriving around the block with his purchases, he threw his eyes in the sky. He just remembered he needed a haircut. His modest flat top had thickened. It needed a quick pass through from Martinez, his barber. Kane tried to be the pretty-boy-type, but fell short. Most of the clothes he owned were his brother's hand-me-downs and some of Dimitri's old things. It wasn't much.

On his way to the barber, nearly off the block, he heard, "Kane, wait up!" It was Tileyah. She sounded like one of the boys. It was cool last week when she didn't take his virginity, but now it irritated him. Actually the sight of her did. He felt that sleeping with her had been a big mistake. She became too attached.

"We need to talk!" she grabbed his hand, turning him around. "Why are you avoiding me? Where are you going now?" She was all set to argue.

Then it hit him.

*They go to the same school. How is this going to work? Tileyah will beat the crap out of Shyla.* Kane, dampened by the thought, went into a dark rage. "Would you stop following me everywhere? I don't like you!" Even as he said the words, they felt wrong. Tileyah dropped back in total disbelief. Trying to apologize, he grabbed for her hand, but was struck twice across the face. She tried to swing again, but Kane managed to grab her wrist.

*Why now, and still on the block for all to see?* Kane muttered to himself. Trying to calm her, he pinned her against Big Eric's new, silver-colored Pathfinder. He took a quick glance up at his window, hoping it was empty. Big Eric was nuts about that Jeep. The last thing he needed was the over-grown behemoth jumping in his face—adding to the mayhem.

Remorseful, Kane whispered in her ear, muttering the word "Sorry" in a soft tone. It didn't work. She was still irate. He was forced to tell her that he loved her. He'd try anything to calm her down. The block loved spectacles.

She relaxed her arms, wiping tears. A half smile crossed her face—questioning if he was really telling the truth. Tileyah had two brothers. She had been around boys through most of her childhood. She was far from stupid, but caved into the idea for the moment.

"Let's talk," Kane said, reaching for her hand. He didn't care about the block finding out about their romance at this point. His first concern was tomorrow; he just wanted that to go well and for that to happen, he had to make sure Tileyah wouldn't see him and Shyla together.

*Think, Kane! Think, Kane! What would my brother do?* In deep thought, he walked with Tileyah up to the barbershop. She had no idea what was going though his wicked mind. Kane always relied on his older brother in times like these.

Then a plan hit him.

"Yo, tomorrow is my birthday. Let's cut at lunch and go to my house. I'll get some Calvin Coolers," Kane suggested, trying to sound excited. Smiling from ear to ear, Tileyah agreed without haste.

"I need to get some money from this dude tomorrow, so I'll meet with you around the back of the building at 1:30." She agreed to everything with a tightened grip around his hand. It was strange to see someone as smart as Tileyah manipulated and so blinded by love.

He felt bad for her, but his guilt faded quickly when he realized that there was a big chance Shyla wouldn't even show up for school anyway. He had options—a great thing to have on his seventeenth birthday.

—

"Pass me that," Cory said, pointing at his pencil, as it rolled under Kane's chair. Finally, it was Friday, Kane's seventeenth birthday, but still there was no sign of Shyla. She normally sat on the other side of the classroom next to the window, giving Kane the perfect view of her. After the school bell rang, he sat, deflated, slowly slouching into his chair. His plan seemingly spoiled.

He sat up quickly, thinking of Tileyah—his plan B. He packed up his things, hoping to meet her at the bus stop.

The front door swung open as a herd of high schoolers made for lunch, Kane in the middle of the crowd.

"Yeah, okay, tomorrow," he responded to Daren. He promised him that he'd play dice tomorrow night, though he had no intentions of returning to 654. Even if that guy was a punk, everyone thought they were invincible on their own block. Besides, Stef mentioned playing dice in a place called The Hole. It was across the street from his building—much closer to home.

In a rapid walk to catch Tileyah, he stopped—surprised. It was Shyla, leaning against the fence near the track field, puffing on a cigarette with her girlfriends. Coming to a complete stop, he parked himself against the railing in front of the school to plan his next move.

*Okay, man relax*, Kane muttered to himself. He stood there trying to build up some courage. Forgetting that Tileyah could be watching his every move, he slowly made his way in Shyla's direction.

"Sup, Shyla? What's up with class?" Kane asked, holding back from choking on the cigarette smoke. Grabbing the attention of the entire crowd, he pulled at his shirt in a sign of nervousness.

"Oh yeah, English. Cory, right?" Shyla answered, turning away from him as she exhaled another plume of smoke.

With a broken smile, he replied, "Yeah, I'm Cory. Let me buy you a beef patty?" Kane was committed to playing it cool and quickly forgave her for getting his name wrong.

She paused shortly then smiled at his new Guess boots. She agreed, but wanted her friends to tag along too. Kane didn't care. Time with Shyla was a dream come true.

After thirty minutes in the bakery.

They ate, laughed, and joked about teachers and students from school. Kane became quite the joker, funnier than normal.

They took their little get-together to her friend's apartment four blocks from the bakery. *I guess this is where she was the past few days*, Kane thought to himself as they headed into Albany project houses. With her friends fading into their own conversation, Kane finally had her all to himself. They talked for nearly an hour before Tileyah crossed his mind.

They tucked themselves in the back room of her friend's apartment. It wasn't long before they began kissing. Shyla wasn't the shy type.

Their tongues continued to twist together. And although he didn't like the stench the Newports left behind, it did not stop him; he was too wrapped up in the moment to care. Her friends, to his surprise, didn't bother looking in their direction. It must have been the norm in the apartment.

Flopping on the bed, she asked abruptly, "Do you have protection?"

"Nah," Kane responded. He never put a condom on in his life, let alone walked around with one in his pocket.

"I'll be right back," Shyla said, walking out of the room. He watched her shapely figure exit. She was beautiful, although the moment wasn't quite what he had imagined. Things were moving so fast. Baffled and anxious, he still wasn't turning her down. He thought of his hygiene teacher, Mr. Albright, saying *"everyone will be sexually active."* The professor was right. This was going to be Kane's second time within a weeks' time and with different girls, no less. His eyes filled with confidence, ready for anything.

⸺

Meanwhile, a slight trickle of rain had begun to fall as Tileyah, tired of standing around waiting, headed to the game room to find shelter. She needed to clear her head. She could not go home or back to school for that matter. Already on punishment for Saturday's stunt with Kane, she began to regret getting involved with him.

Moments later, she entered the game room. It was packed as usual, with high schoolers and some older kids. Lenny's Arcade Room, although occasionally raided by the police, had good lookouts—making it one of the premier cut spots.

"Dimitri!" Tileyah said, shocked. "What are you doing here?" She smiled in amusement, waiting for an answer as she leaned against the new Mrs. Pac Man game. Dimitri, for the most part, was a good student. You had to beg him to cut school most times.

Grinning from ear to ear, he said that he wanted to play the new Punch Out game. Everyone was talking about it. After a while, she forgot about Kane, filling her time watching Dimitri struggle to get off the second level of Punch Out.

Back at the apartment.

Shyla had returned with a condom, pulled from her girlfriend's back pocket. She closed the door behind her, grinning.

Hours passed.

Walking towards the window, Kane fixed his blue and white striped colored boxers. They were high up—twenty-one floors. He could see the twin towers in Manhattan even with the dense fog. Turning around to get a glimpse at her, he sat on the radiator next to the window. Her ass protruded through the ruffled sheets. She rolled around and looked up at him, twisting her lips. She looked extra cute every time she did that and she knew it. None of his dreams came close to this.

*I should have waited,* Kane thought to himself. He deeply regretted sleeping with Tileyah now so more than ever. He walked towards the bed, collecting his pants from the floor. "Oh, my name is—" Shyla interrupted, "Kane. I know stupid." She tugged at his waist for a kiss.

He liked her. She was funny and prettier than Tileyah—more experienced. He just wished she wouldn't smoke; it didn't suit her pretty face. Besides cigarette smoke always reminded him of his father. He could not stand the slightest hint of it.

He fastened his belt, preparing to go, as he heard a few new voices entering the apartment. "Where are you going?" Shyla asked. He glanced at the clock. "It's getting late. Her parents will be back, right?" Kane questioned. She explained that her friend's parents would not be back until tomorrow. They went out of town for a funeral. Her absence from school for those three days made sense now.

"Come," she said as she pulled him out of the bedroom into the crowded living room. Kane did not like the idea of strange guys around. He immediately gazed over at the front door. He was almost certain one of them was going to flirt with Shyla, and fighting alone in Albany housing projects would have been risky. They were one of the worst projects in Brooklyn.

Cautiously, following Shyla into the living room, he found four guys slumped across the sofa with forty-ounce bottles of Ole English carefully placed at their feet. They were all laughing at a taped *In Living Color* episode.

"Hey Kev, Trace, this is Kane" Shyla shouted over the TV. They looked older—twenty perhaps. They nodded their heads, gesturing hello, but never giving him any real attention. Kane was completely uncomfortable and with the fog darkening the sky, he really felt the urge to leave.

He pulled her back into the bedroom "I gotta run. I need to pick up this money." It was Kane's favorite line. It was an easy lie because people usually owed him money from his dice games.

She shook her head. "You're not leaving right now, sorry." He thought she was kidding and waited for a smile or something. No such luck. Her face remained the same way as she made her way back towards the living room. He knew at this point that he was going to stay. Shyla had an overpowering personality and he liked her too much to upset her. He went back to the window, grabbing another peek at Manhattan and the fading skyline. He waited for her to return to the bedroom.

Suddenly, he heard, "Here we go yo, Here we go yo…!" It was an explosion of a *Tribe Called Quest's Scenario* song. It came from the living room. It vibrated the walls throughout the apartment. He loved that song. He remained fixed at the window rapping against the beat with some lyrics that he and Craig had come up with last summer.

Shyla returned moments later holding a full 40-ounce bottle of Ole English then shut the door behind her. From that moment, he knew he would do everything to keep her. She understood he didn't want to mingle with the crowd and didn't force the issue. And although she didn't live up to the timid girl in his dreams, reality was much better.

Kane never had Ole English before, but today he made an exception.

Shyla passed him the bottle with a huge grin on her face—as if she knew it was his first time drinking the stuff. He took the top off like a pro; he'd seen it done a hundred times. He put the bottle to his mouth and started guzzling. The taste was harsh, as he suspected, but ice cold as well, killing some of the bad after taste. They both took turns drinking from the bottle. Kane, loved her boyish ways, it came off very attractive.

Suddenly there was a knock at the front door.

More people entered the apartment. It quickly turned into a full-blown house party. She immediately got up and locked the bedroom door, taking her blouse off. Grinning from ear to ear, trying to keep cool, he took another sip from the bottle as he flopped on the bed.

Feeling the buzz from the malt liquor, he pulled her towards the bed, completely confident. He never felt this drunk before. He flipped her across the bed, throwing himself on top of her. He stopped abruptly, smiling, as the DJ decided to play "When I'm with you" by Toney Terry. The timing couldn't have been any better. It was the most popular love song out at the moment. He glared down into her eyes, serious, and then crested her hair. He was all set to tell her how he felt, but immediately pulled away reaching for the bottle. Kane was never good at expressing himself that way. Better, for him, she'd probably take it as a sign of weakness. Shyla didn't seem like she'd be turned on by guys expressing themselves that way.

They never left the bedroom as the party progressed through the night. There was not a single knock on the door. They drank, talked, kissed, and then made love for the rest of the night.

The morning's sunlight pierced through the beige-colored shades. He awoke naked, with her resting on his chest with the bed sheets hanging off the bedside. After a series of twisting and turning, they both decided to get up. *Beautiful, even in the morning,* he thought, looking down on her as he tried to locate his pants.

"Did you use a condom?" Shyla worried as she quickly pulled the sheet over her body and stood up. Her expression said it all, filled with nerves—bothered by her carelessness. They both were stone drunk, tied up in the heat of the moment. They did not use protection after the first time that afternoon. Kane barely remembered anything. "Nah, but you're good. I was careful," he said. He put on a serious face and did his best to reassure her.

"Her parents are coming soon, so…." Shyla opened the bedroom door, to let Kane out. He knew she was upset and didn't bother asking her for her number to call later. He'd see her in class perhaps. He put on his hooded sweater, tucked his head down and headed out.

He didn't think anything of it; she was more upset at herself than with him. Shyla was a smart girl, but loved the streets more. She came from a decent family. She told him how her parents had died in a car accident in East Orange, New Jersey; forcing her to live in Brooklyn with her grandparents in Flatbush. Her grandparents, for the most part, were pushovers, and let her do whatever she wanted, as long as she had a half-decent excuse. But she seemed to know where her limits were and getting pregnant was one of them.

He took the bus, hung-over, but happy. It was easily the best birthday he'd ever had. Finally, through all the countless dreams, reality finally made its way into his life. He gazed out of the window on the B12 bus, resurrecting moments from the night before.

The air felt clean—new, and carried a fresh smell of spring through the crack of the window. He took it all in. He rang the bell to exit the bus, deciding to walk the rest of the way home. After grabbing a few Debbie Cakes and a pineapple juice from the corner store, he decided to watch a three on three basketball game at Patterson Park. He missed playing—especially with Dimitri and even with Tileyah for that matter. Tileyah. He sighed, finally it fully crossed his mind that he stood her up. *What am I going to tell her?* Kane thought to himself.

Kane slouched off the side of the bench, his body still uneven from the night before. An hour later, he lifted himself up, then headed home.

# Chapter Four

T HE PHONE RANG FROM THE KITCHEN. Kane was sound asleep with his bedroom door closed shut.

"Kane, the phone! It's your sister, again." His mother set the phone next to his door. She was still fuming that he spent the night out on Friday. He had slept the weekend away, stayed in bed mostly and vowed never to drink Ole English again.

"Alright!" he answered sharply and jumped down from the bunk bed. He began to hate his house and took it out on his mother with muttered, one-word responses. His house seemed to be filled with ghosts that were waiting for them to leave. It had an eerie emptiness to it that he always wanted to get away from.

"Hey," Jade shouted, "I've been calling all weekend! It's Sunday already." He loved the fact that she wanted to wish him a happy birthday. When Kane was younger, she'd put penny candies under his pillow and wrote "Happy Birthday Kanie" on construction paper taken from her art class. He loved her. She called once a week to check on the house, although they never managed a conversation over two minutes.

"Happy Birthday, Kanie! What's new?" Jade asked, pausing for a quick second before continuing, "Oh and make sure you help Mommy around the house." He heard the same questions and requests from her nearly each week, but didn't snub it off today.

"Shyla and some friends threw me a small party," Kane exaggerated the news. His sister asked a ton of questions, about his party and Shyla. He answered all of them, mostly with lies, especially about the drinking and sex.

Jade always managed to extract from him a promise to clean something around the house. Kane made a half-hearted attempt to clean the bathroom, leaving behind an untouched bathtub, along with a layer of dust on the mirror. He just wanted to get outdoors. He hadn't stepped outside all weekend, and could hear people playing basketball on the side of the building.

He threw the sponge beneath the sink and headed for the front door.

Minutes later.

"That's ten!" Lionel said, walking back to the foul line. The entire crew was out: Dimitri, Stef, Lionel and some guys from the 234 building. Even Tileyah was there watching the game sitting on a cheap black and red Michael Jordan basketball.

*Tileyah.* Kane paused when he saw her, but then continued heading towards the basketball game. *It was a good time as any to conjure up a fresh set of lies for her.* He leaned against the tree around the foul line. He was in full view and waited to catch her eye.

*Nothing.*

He knew now that she was ignoring him. It was for the best. It made it easier. He turned towards the game, placing his hands in his pocket.

"That's me!" Stef called out for a foul after a disorganized lay up to the basket. Kane always hated when Stef played, he always managed to interrupt the game with petty complaints and false calls. Kane could have had the game after next, but decided to watch from the side instead. He watched for hours. He even watched Tileyah play a few games. He felt bad each time she got the ball. He realized that he lost a good friend—and lover for that matter, because of his stupidity. Tileyah never approached him. Her face remained fixed straight the entire time.

Thirty minutes later, the game ended and Stef headed off the court.

"Yo, Stef! Wait up," Kane yelled, jogging along beside him. He wanted to know when Stef was going to shoot dice down in The Hole again. Kane dreaded the idea of possibly hanging out with him, but was out of options. After giving Kane lip for ten minutes, Stef said, he'd be at The Hole tonight.

"I'll knock on your door when I go," he added. He headed upstairs; Kane followed after. He hadn't done homework all week and promised himself that he would at least put something down on paper. School had become a huge problem, even before his father's death. It really started when his sister left the house. At the rate he was going, dropping out before his senior year was likely. He'd grown tired of thinking of the future and of listening to Mr. Albright's endless questions about his grades. The man would constantly hound him about what he wanted to do with life. Kane always replied, "*I need to survive the hood first, and then I can think about being something.*" At this point, Kane did just enough work to stay in the classroom. His grades were now terrible in every class, even science, his favorite.

Hours later.

His textbooks and a spiral notebook fell from his bunk bed to the floor. He'd fallen asleep inside his biology text book. He sat up and checked the window. *Shit! It's dark!* Kane jumped down from his bed and headed for the kitchen to check the time. "Nine-thirty! *Fucking Stef! Why do I even bother with him?*" Kane mumbled beneath his breath.

The smell of baked chicken and fresh sweet potatoes, escaped from the oven as he headed back to his room to get dressed. His mother always cooked on Sundays out of habit. When he was young, they'd eat together after church every Sunday. However, these days he was more interested in playing dice than sitting down with his mother for dinner. Moments later, he made for the front door without entertaining even a quick bite to go.

His mother remained quiet, didn't question his late night expeditions. Every day, she became more detached. Ironically, her cooking had gotten much better, though Kane was too distracted to notice. Sometimes he wished that she'd challenge him, to show some interest in his life, but he didn't know how sick she had become.

The front of the building was empty. For the first time, he was disappointed not to see Stef out in front of the building. He decided to walk to The Hole by himself.

He didn't bother knocking on Dimitri's door to ask him along. Aside from all the other reasons, Dimitri didn't like gambling. He was a hard-core video gamer. Kane; however, wasn't good at Mrs. Pac Man or Centipede. He'd never gotten pass the second board. He felt the entire thing was a waste of money.

*The Hole.*

The mere thought of actually going down there by himself made him tighten up in nervousness. He slowly walked up towards it. The

Hole was the only place in the hood with a basketball court you had to walk down large cement steps to reach. From afar, you could make out the top portions of the backboard, but never the chaos going on at the bottom. People from his block rarely traveled there, especially at night. The Hole was only a five-minute walk from his building, but had one of the worst reputations for shoot-outs, drugs, and robberies. Many people came to The Hole during the day to play organized basketball games, but at night, it belonged to the thugs from buildings 565 and 568. Everyone knew that.

*I'll just take a quick look around for Stef, and then I'll leave,* Kane thought to himself. He put his foot on the top step and stared down into the crowd.

"Give me my money, motherfucker!" Some guy pulled at another guy's pocket playfully, but partly serious. Sometimes it was difficult to tell. Kane couldn't believe his eyes. The Hole was packed with people—girls and guys. He counted six games of dice, and then stopped as he saw Stef in the distance. He recognized that loud, orange jump suit he'd wear to school nearly every day. He headed towards the closest dice game. Hanging around Stef could be dangerous in a place like this.

It was extremely dark—darker than any dice game he'd ever played in. The only lights offered came from cigarettes, blunts, gold links, and one brightly-lit equalizer coming from a 12" box radio blasting Wu-Tang at the bottom of the steps. Kane only had ten dollars but still felt like he was in heaven. He looked on quietly, trying to keep from smiling.

"This yours?" Some stranger inquired, moving a half-empty 40 ounce bottle of Ole English off to the side. Kane looked at him and quickly shook his head. *No.* The whole place was strange, but he loved it. He sat there, feeling calm; marveling at the site. *These are the real gangsters,* he thought, more impressed than fearful. He gazed around at the abundance of gold shining through their white suede jumpers and their freshly bought sneakers. *This is heaven*, he thought, breaking into a silent grin.

"Yo, you playing?" Some guy asked. Kane shook his head. *No*, he didn't want to play just yet. He was still taking in the scene. He leaned back, looking to see if Stef was still around.

Twenty minutes passed.

The game ended. "Yo! I got next!" Kane said, trying to speak over the music.

"Yo, Shorty, the bank is twenty-five dollars. You got that?" One of the guys asked, holding the dice. Kane nodded his head yes, as the guy passed him the dice, smiling.

Kane prayed for a six or seven as he rolled the dice against the steps. A six or a seven would have put him in a great position to win, anything less would push his score down. Crap, a four. He lucked out on his first roll.

"Don't worry bout it," one of the players yelled out, making Kane comfortable in an instant—a big difference from that idiot from 654. It was clear these guys had money. They seemed to be playing dice for the hell of it. Even when they lost money, they smiled about it.

"Wow, Shorty is doing his thing," yelled the same guy who had passed Kane the dice thirty minutes ago. Kane had won three games already, was up fifty-five dollars and was trying for more. It took everything to keep from smiling.

"What's your name, shorty?" The same guy asked, as Kane grabbed the dice from the asphalt. It was his roll again, but Kane had begun to sense that the game was ending because most of the players had started to turn their attention to the girls coming down the steps on the other side. Breaking off from a dice game like that in any other place would have resulted in an instant fight, but there was no way in hell Kane was about to take issue with it.

"Kay," Kane replied to the guy, trying not to stare at him for too long. "Yo, I'm Justice," he reached out for a handshake. He seemed friendly; laid back as if he had it all. He wore fresh, green and white Stan Smith Adidas, an untouched white suede Nautica suit topped with a huge gold link chain. Kane knew this guy didn't need the fifty-five dollars he'd just lost, so he immediately dismissed the notion that Justice was plotting to take it back from him. Kane listened as his newfound friend went on about who was really getting money in The Hole. Justice pointed out all the gangsters and robbers. He kept calling Kane "Shorty," even though Justice only seemed a few years older and was slightly shorter.

Commotion from the other side of the basketball court caught the attention of everyone who stood around after the dice game.

"Don't walk away from me, bitch!" Some guy yelled as he jogged after some helpless girl. They headed for the top steps. "I'll kill you!"

Suddenly, a chilling sound rung across the court.

The music went silent.

He punched her.

The poor girl fell to the ground, as he continued to pummel her face.

He continued on, bashing her face against the bottom edge of the concrete step.

"Yo, come on Ant! What the fuck, man!" a voice yelled in the distance as a few guys finally decided to pull him off the poor woman. *Ant?* Kane wondered if that was Big Ant, the same guy who had a beef with his brother.

"This dude," Justice said, smiling. He pulled out a pack of cigarettes as if it was okay. But it wasn't okay, at least not for Kane. His father would occasionally go into drunken fits, putting his hands on his mother.

With much of The Hole gathering around to see the fight, it was a good time to leave. "I'm out, man," Kane said, giving Justice a five. As he took his hand, he knew he'd be back. Kane had a new spot to play dice with high rollers who laughed off their losses.

Weeks went by.

Shyla wasn't pregnant. Kane's schoolwork worsened and he took to cutting class every chance he could. Anything to be with Shyla. He'd gotten used to the aftertaste 40 ounces of Ole English left behind, even though he'd vowed never to drink it again. He'd made constant trips to The Hole, money or not. If he wasn't playing dice, he was laughing it up and drinking with Justice.

"Mr. Davis!" Mr. Albright waved Kane over. Kane knew it was time for one of his speeches. He grimaced. He wasn't in the mood. He was hung over from last night. Justice bought everyone their own 40 ounce of Ole English. There were rumors that he had robbed someone. Usually, he had plenty of stories to tell, but last night he had quickly changed the subject when asked where the money came from.

"What do you want from life son?" Mr. Albright sat on the edge of the desk as he started his inquiry. Kane liked Mr. Albright; he grew up in the neighborhood and knew how things were. Kane would listen to him only because he didn't pretend to know it all.

"You are smart enough to know that you are failing this class and, from what I hear, most of your other classes as well." Kane sat, listening, as he preached about the hood, being killed and having a career. Fifteen minutes went by with much of his words going in one ear and out the other. Kane was fixated on Shyla and only had an interest in drinking 40 ounces, and hanging out with Justice in The Hole. To him, he didn't need anything else.

Mr. Albright mentioned a few times that Kane could be an engineer if he applied himself. He was once a good student of math and science.

"Okay, Mr. Albright. Okay…" he responded as he exited the room. *An engineer?* Really, he thought. It was the first time he had heard anything like that. Mr. Albright always said something to motivate him. For the next few days, he made an honest attempt to get back on track, but then quickly realized he was too far behind. Life seemed much easier without school.

A month later. His grades plummeted to their worst levels.

The school year was over and it was either summer school or the eleventh grade again. He decided that he was not taking summer school.

There was a knock at Kane's door.

He answered it, surprised.

It was Dimitri. They had drifted so far apart. They barely saw each other nowadays.

"Yo, we're going to see New Jack City? Wanna go?" Dimitri asked, excited. "Man, I'm going with my girl," Kane replied as if Dimitri would be impressed. "Maybe I'll see ya over there. Going to 42nd Street?" Kane continued. Kane had no plans to go to the movies. He was heading to The Hole to meet up with Justice. It was the clearest sign that their friendship was shifting further apart – a sad revelation. Dimitri had been his friend all his life. He knew Kane had started hanging with Justice and hated the idea that he was in The Hole nearly every night. His invite was his way of trying to pull Kane away from that. *No such luck.*

Later on at The Hole

"That was a seven, motherfucker!" Justice shouted from a corner, as Kane fixed himself to the voice and made his way down the steps. He was getting closer to Justice and a few of his other friends, but their friendship only existed inside The Hole. They never went further than the corner store together.

"Yo, Kay! You in?" asked Justice, drunk already. He stumbled over to greet him. Kane told him he was not playing dice today—maybe tomorrow. However, he knew he wouldn't have money until next week when the check came or so his mother kept telling him. She barely spent time at the house these days. Between his sloppiness and bad attitude, he noticed that she was staying over at her sister, Dorothy's house more often. He'd find himself calling over there to see when she was coming home.

"What's the bank?" questioned Kane as he leaned against a pole; frustrated. He was tired of being broke and was beginning to get tired of playing dice. He was considering working at Burger King or Wendy's on Pitkin Avenue, but Troy from his music class said that they had stopped hiring summer help two weeks ago.

Suddenly.

The sound of a car screeching to a halt echoed throughout the basketball court.

It rolled up to the front steps. It wasn't until the headlights flicked on that Kane knew it was a black Buick with tinted windows. His heart began pounding as he turned around.

More sounds of rubber screeched loudly against the pavement.

Another car pulled up at the top of the steps, right in Kane's direction. Before he could make a run for it, he saw a white man jump out of the front seat with a silver badge dangling from his chest.

"Cops!" Kane yelled out, stating the obvious. Kane really had no reason to run, but he did anyway. "Shit! Shit!" he recognized the voice behind him. It was Justice. "Kay! Kay! Here...take it, take it!" He tried to pass Kane a silver-plated 9mm, a shiny-looking handgun for all to see. Kane frowned, conflicted, but had no time to think about it. His first thought was of Justice. If he was arrested and charged with that gun, there's no telling how he would take it. It was a rift Kane didn't want to deal with. In an instant, he wiped the gun clean from Justice's hands and threw it in his front pocket.

Kane heard a tumble.

Justice tripped and fell behind him. The usually on point gangster was too drunk to keep up. As Kane started up the steps again, he saw plain-clothes cops grabbing for anyone in sight. Finally, up at the top step, he made for building 565. He was certain Justice had been arrested by now.

He sprinted for dear life and didn't look back. He entered the building and headed for the stairwell. He could sense that cops were behind him.

*Where to go?* Kane wondered frantically. He didn't know anyone in the building. He ran up to the second floor, stopping to catch his breath in the stairwell.

The stench of urine in the stairwell forced him out into the hallway. It was empty.

*Thank God!* He sighed. He peeked out the hallway window, in search of the police.

Nothing.

Suddenly, the front door crashed open.

Kane heard the sound of keys jingling and feet shuffling. The police. They headed up the stairs. Panic rose in Kane's throat like vomit.

He paced back and forth, looking for a place to hide the gun. He considered the incinerator, but it was jammed full. The cops were sure to find it there.

The jingling of keys grew closer.

He ducked behind the stairwell door.

The noise reached the second floor.

The police were on the other side of the door. Riddled with fear, he prayed, as if God should consider saving him from his stupidity.

"We got him!" Another cop shouted in a distance. Another poor soul ran into the building, but was not so lucky. Kane sighed in relief as the cops made their way back down the steps with the unlucky teen. He looked up, as if God had something to do with his sudden string of luck.

He kept himself by the window for two hours before heading down the steps and out the building. The Hole and most of the surrounding blocks were empty. Walking back to his block, he overheard a couple of girls talking, "Yeah, some cop got shot earlier, so they raided everything."

Moments later.

"Wow," Kane gasped. He flopped down on the bottom bunk, his brother's old bed. He was so grateful he had made it home safely. He had been so terrified that he almost forgot about the gun, until now.

Kane pulled it out in amazement. A *9mm pistol—seemingly brand new and sliver plated!* It was a beautiful looking gun. He pointed it at the mirror. It felt like a new toy. He twirled it around for a good thirty minutes, before placing it in his old sneaker box. His mother hadn't come in his room since his father died. It was unlikely she'd find it there.

*Oh, Shyla is coming over tomorrow; I better clean up a bit*, he thought to himself. Picking up his clothes, he thought about Justice. He knew

Justice was arrested and wondered when he should return to The Hole. He wondered if Justice had drugs on him and hoped he had enough time to ditch them. Kane thought about waiting until Friday before taking a walk back there.

Two weeks passed.

Kane returned to The Hole nearly every night, but did not see Justice or any of his boys. In fact, The Hole remained empty since the day after the raid. Kane thought about the gun. As much as he marveled over it, he wanted to give it back. He was sure Justice wanted it. *What gangster wouldn't?*

"Where are you going?" Shyla asked, turning towards him as he was pulling up his jeans. She had been at his house for a week now. He needed some air. He figured he'd take a quick peek around The Hole for Justice, and then head for Poppies' corner store for some junk food.

"I'm going to the store," he said. "Want something?" He wanted to dash out before Shyla started in with her interrogation.

"You're leaving? Now? If you're not back in fifteen minutes, I'm leaving." She turned her back towards him and collected the bed sheet from the floor. He did not bother to argue. They'd been bickering all week; sounding more and more like a married couple.

Music was playing in the distance as Kane made his way to The Hole.

Finally, there were a few dice games going on, but still no sign of Justice. Kane never liked asking for Justice when he wasn't around. He was sure to have enemies. In the hood, asking for the wrong person could get you killed. Kane was always careful about that kind of thing. Looking around, he spotted another game carefully tucked in the far corner. No doubt, they were smoking more than cigarettes as the soft breeze carried the stench of weed to his nose.

Carefully approaching the game, he softly leaned against the pole, eyeing in. *They're just kids*, he realized. One looked no older than twelve, and the rest were, perhaps nine or ten. The twelve year old put the joint behind his back.

"Yo, you know Justice?" Kane questioned them softly. Although they were just kids, Kane knew to keep himself humbled. Most of the time it was kids their age doing the dirty work for some of the drug dealers.

"Justice? With the black Pathfinder?" One of the younger kids asked.

"Yeah," Kane replied. No one could get Justice to stop talking about the problems he had with that Jeep. Although Kane had never seen it, he'd heard that it looks better than it runs.

"Yeah. I saw him earlier. Check 565, they be playing dice on the side," the boy answered, turning back to the game. As Kane thanked him, he realized that 565 was the same building where he'd nearly been arrested. It was one of the worst buildings in the projects. He didn't run into danger that night, mainly because the police had chased away all the troublemakers. He collected his nerves and gingerly started towards the building.

He had left the gun at home, in fear of another raid. His heart started racing, as he approached the front door. Five guys at the front entrance had their eyes glued on him. They all paused—cautious—waiting for his first words. A motion too quick or too slow would have surely cost him his life.

Fear had strangled his words, but he needed to speak.

"Yo," Kane said. "What up? You seen Justice?" He tried to keep control of his fear. It took everything he had not to seem nervous.

"Who the fuck is you?" One of the guys asked swiftly, stepping down off the steps. He made his way towards Kane.

Oh. *What a big mistake.* Kane glanced over at the fence, preparing to run.

"Oh shit, that's Kay," another guy yelled out as he jumped in front. Sighing in relief, Kane couldn't help but smile. He failed to conceal his nervousness; his hand was noticeable twitching. They laughed it off and continued talking.

"Yo, Justice was looking for you. Yo, you got that right?" the guy said, throwing his arms around Kane as they started around the side of the building. Kane quickly explained everything, telling him that he'd been checking The Hole every day, but nothing.

"Yo, Justice look who I found," the guy said to Justice excited. Kane never knew his name, but he'd seen him around The Hole and remembered that his dice skills were terrible.

Justice turned around.

"Yo, you got that, right?" Justice asked, with a worried look.

"Yeah, yeah, I was telling—"

Justice cut him off as soon as the word "yeah" left Kane's mouth.

"This is a true gangster right here!" Justice grabbed at Kane's head, then leaned back, smiling against the fence as Kane went through his story of that night. He even talked about running up to the second floor, but left out the part about him shivering uncontrollably in the hallway; praying for a miracle. The fifteen minutes Shyla gave him were up, but there was no way he was about to leave.

They headed to Poppies for some 40 ounces of malt liquor—any kind would do. He was relieved to see Justice. He also wanted to get some closure with the gun. Justice was locked up for nearly two weeks. The police wanted him to participate in a lineup. Most of the plain-clothes cops knew Justice, but they'd never caught him red-handed with anything, at least not yet. Kane listened to his story in amazement and felt good he had a small war story of his own to brag about.

"Yo, Kay," Justice said, pulling him away from the crowd. "Bring it tomorrow, I live in 12F. Yo really, I like what you did. Some real soldier shit." He then asked Kane quietly, "Yo, anyone dealing in your building?"

"Listen, and check around. I don't want any beef, but if it's clean then I want you to start working for me. It's getting too hot over here." He grabbed Kane's head playfully. Kane didn't know if anyone was selling in his building, but promised he'd find out. The thought of working for Justice was appealing. People respected him and they feared him.

Hours passed.

Most of the crew left. Only Justice, Kane, and Keys remained. Keys was one of Justice's main workers. They had lived in the same building since they were kids.

"Yo, Kay. Hold this," Justice passed him a handful of cash. Kane was confused until Justice smiled and said, "You earned it."

Another smile broke from Kane's face as he waved them off, shouting, "Tomorrow!" *What a night*, he thought, as he turned the corner towards home. He couldn't wait to see how much money he had.

"*20, 40, 60, 80…*100 dollars!" Kane shouted down the street. He could not believe it. Just like that, Justice handed him a hundred dollars. He approached his front door and hoped Shyla had gone home. He was drunk and just wanted to sleep. It was a good night and he didn't want it spoiled with another fight.

As he opened the door, he realized that Shyla was still there. His bedroom door was closed with the TV playing. He retired to the living room, flopping on the green suede sofa.

The next day.

"Yo, Kay! Come in!" Justice waved Kane into his apartment, wearing the same clothes from yesterday. The house was nearly empty and unfurnished. The kitchen table was filled with unwashed pots. Every corner of the living room was littered with 40-ounce bottles; some of them half full. The apartment was covered in filth, with dirty clothes thrown everywhere.

"Yo, wait here," Justice said as he headed to the back. Kane wisely sat on the edge of the chair in the kitchen, trying to spare his nose the wretched smell of dirty socks and stale booze. It was strange that Justice, a person known to have money, couldn't find a way to keep his apartment cleaner than what it was. Kane immediately thought of his apartment and hoped it would never come to this. He vowed to clean up a little later when he got home. Moving the pots aside, he carefully placed the gun on the table. He didn't want to stay long. He'd promised Shyla a date to go see the New Jack City movie, before it left the theaters. He also wanted to make up for last night.

"Yo," Justice shouted, returning with a cigarette in his left ear; hair uncombed. He was a regular bad boy—a pure street hustler. Although Kane took to his deep ruggedness, there was something about the moment that made him uncomfortable. He preferred their dice games and listening to his war stories at the bottom of The Hole. Maybe it was the apartment that made him uneasy.

Kane listened patiently while Justice explained how he wanted to start dealing over by Kane's block. His building was getting hot with the cops. Kane nodded as Justice explained the situation. He talked about how much Kane could make; further trying to sell the idea. Nearly thirty minutes had passed and Kane felt like he was ready to start selling drugs immediately. Justice had that way of talking people into things. Despite the way he kept his apartment, he was highly organized when it came to selling drugs.

Kane agreed to everything, but knew he had to give it more thought. The money would be a good thing. He would have nice clothes on a regular basis and maybe he'd even get the chance to buy that new equalizer he was dying for. However, he knew it was illegal and that his family would not approve, namely Jade.

Kane left the apartment feeling confused about life. He thought of Mr. Albright's words, "*You can be an engineer.*" He frowned as he walked home to collect Shyla. There was so much to think about in so little time. Justice liked Kane. Kane could decline his offer and still keep him as a friend. The pressure was solely on Kane himself.

As he approached his front door, a fresh smell of Pine Sol seeped from beneath it. *Man, my mother is home cleaning. Shit.* He liked it when it was just him and Shyla at home. He sighed then opened the door.

Relieved, a smile crept across his face. There she was—Shyla— vigorously passing a mop across the kitchen floor. The house was nearly clean and a soft breeze drifted in from the kitchen window adding to the pleasant surprise. He took off his sweater and started to help. After leaving Justice's, he could have cleaned the entire house.

After a few minutes working with the sponge, Kane pulled her over by the waist. Turned on by her pink, tight shorts, he tried to pull her in the bedroom.

"No, no, no. We are going to the movies, Kay," Shyla said in a serious tone. She was smart enough to know that if they started making love, there would be no end in sight. With much of the apartment clean, they stepped out and headed for the number 3 train up to 42nd Street where New Jack City was waiting from them.

The movie finished and a crowd of people headed for the exit. Kane leaned against the side wall near the women's bathroom, waiting for Shyla. He was still absorbing the movie. *Nino Brown, man.* Scenes from the movie swirled around in his head. It was clear now what he would tell Justice. The excitement and energy from Nino Brown and the CMB crew reminded him of life with Justice. Ignoring the fact that Nino Brown was a no-good drug dealer who killed his best friend in the movie, Kane still gravitated to his character. His decision was final. He didn't have to mull things over anyone.

Two weeks passed.

The night was windy and dark. It felt more like fall than summer. Cold, Kane rubbed the back of his arms, fighting the chill from the wind. Around the side of the building, he sat on top of the bench, waiting for his first customer. Justice had explained everything and had even given him an old, fully loaded 9mm handgun. His leg twitched in nervousness as a dark shadow approached. *A cop*, he thought. He took a quick glance at the drug-filled paper bag near the tree, ensuring it was out of sight. He stood anxiously, holding his 9mm against the front of his waist, wondering if he should try to dispose of it.

This is too risky, he thought as the shadows emerged from the darkness. Quickly jumping down from the bench, Kane was all ready to make a run for it and leave the drugs behind, but then he recognized the shadows. It was Stef and some other dude.

"Yo, what the fuck you doing out here?" Stef asked, smiling as he made his way to sit on the bench.

"Yo, yo, you can't stay here!" Kane retorted, irritated by the site of him.

"What? Get the fuck out of here," Stef sat on the edge of the bench and pulled a blunt from behind his ear.

Stef had aggravated Kane ever since they were kids. Normally, the very sight of him made Kane aggravated, but now, with a gun at his waist, Kane was enraged.

"Yo," Kane said, pulling the gun from his waist. "Yo, this is Justice's new spot. Ya can't stay here!" Kane raised his voice, giving Stef a blistering stare. He held out his gun and pointed it to the ground, making sure Stef took notice. Stef's eyes widened as he slowly made his way off the bench.

"The fuck you going to do with that?" Stef asked, trying to hide his nervousness. He looked into Kane's icy glare and continued to distance himself away from the bench. Everyone that came close to The Hole knew the name "Justice" and what it meant to have a beef with him.

Kane tucked his gun away and headed back to the bench. They walked away, mumbling about how Kane wasn't a real gangster. Maybe he wasn't. Maybe he wasn't yet, but in the heat of the moment, he sure seemed like one.

Another shadow approached from the opposite side. Still angry, he stared in silence, watching the shadow approach. It was a drug user for sure. The dirty smell of the streets reached him before she did. *She was too young to be doing crack.* Only twenty or so, perhaps. Her clothes were dirty and outdated. He had seen bums on the streets, even some drug users, but she looked different. She seemed more desperate with wide-opened eyes and an off-balanced walk. He pulled the gun from his waist and headed for the brown paper bag.

"Yo, tell your friends to come see me, Kay." He sat back on the bench as he watched her walk back into the blackness. It was his first drug sale. His life as a criminal had started.

# Chapter Five

MONTHS WENT BY.
Business was great all summer. Hard core drug users were coming all the way from East New York to see Kane. Justice thought it best for Kane to have a partner, so he sent Keys to help. Keys, a laid back guy, quiet most of the time whom loved to rhyme. The two of them got along right away. If they weren't selling crack, they were rapping over instrumental songs at Kane's house. It seemed Keys was more interested in rapping than making it big in the drug business. Kane, on the other hand, was gravitating to the drug life. It was still about clothes and sneakers for him, and impressing Shyla, of course. They were still a couple, but since school had begun they'd seen each other mostly on the weekends.

It had been a magical summer for Kane. He had the latest of everything and had even bought a new gold link chain similar to Justice's. Justice became more of a boss than a friend to him, but the business was growing and Kane began making a name for himself.

A fierce wind blew a chunk of leaves from the trees. It was getting late. Kane only had five vials left. A familiar drug user approached. It was trusty old Henry Head. Keys and Kane always poked fun at him. He was an old, experienced drug user. Always good for something comedic.

"Give me twenty large, Kay," the underweight drug user said, passing Kane a handful of dirty single bills. Sighing in frustration, Kane quickly grabbed the money and started his count. He wanted to go upstairs. Keys had left an hour ago; he was bored and tired of the cold.

"Listen," he said to Henry, carefully passing him the drugs, "Tell them I'm at 6-E." He pointed at his building.

Hours later, Kane and his mother were sound asleep. It was 3:30am. Suddenly, a loud bang came from the front door. It had awakened his mother. She jumped up startled. She made her way to the peephole. She saw a strange man who was under-dressed for this time of year. He wore a dirty orange t-shirt and jeans blackened from dirt and oil. The stranger paced back and forth, itching his head anxiously. He made for another strike. His vibrating kick sent her back in total fright. She ran to the back to collect her only protection.

"Kane, Kane!" she said, bursting into his room frantically. "Someone is trying to break in!"

Kane jumped down from his bed and tried to remember where he'd put his gun.

*Under the mattress.*

He developed the bad habit of reaching for it at the first sign of trouble. He left it this time, out of respect for his mother.

The stranger struck the door again, this time louder than before. Kane headed for the door, slightly edgy but calm for the most part. *If it's the police, I can throw the gun through the window along with the two vials of crack I have left,* he thought. After dealing for months, Justice had taught him everything he needed to know about not getting caught.

The door continued to tremble with every kick. Kane finally reached the peephole. "Shit!" He shouted in aggravation. He remembered telling Henry Head he lived in apartment 6E. What a mistake! What was he thinking? They'll knock all night thinking his apartment was a crack spot. "Shit," he said again, anxious.

He turned and saw his mother dialing the police. "No, no," he said, pulling the phone from her. He explained quickly that the disgruntled customer was his friend Keys' uncle and that he was holding some money for the man. Agitated, he made for his bedroom in search of the two crack vials.

Kane opened the front door and headed out into the hall, fuming. "What the fuck? Are you fucking—" Kane said, grabbing the poor soul by the neck as they walked away from his front door. It took everything he had not to punch the poor man in the face.

"I need three young blood. Look what I got for you," the desperate patron pleaded as he pulled out a fake gold watch and three dollars. Kane, too worried about his mother calling the police, gave him the last of the drugs as he made his way back inside.

"Kane!" his mother yelled, staring at three empty crack vials she had placed on the table. "Are you selling drugs?" Her voice cracked with disappointment.

"No. Where did you get that from?" Kane asked, angry that she had been in his room and had gone through his things. He snatched them from the table as he headed for his room.

"It's Keys'," he yelled after slamming his bedroom door shut.

Twenty minutes later. He heard another knock at the front door again. He jumped off his bed. He had a good idea who it was—another crack user. After he explained to the foul-smelling woman that his apartment was not a crack spot, he went downstairs to wait for the next desperate soul. It took Kane two weeks to straighten out that mess.

—

After making his first thousand dollars this past summer, he knew he wasn't returning to school. A tragic decision for such a promising science student. He still made his way around the area, because of Shyla. Their relationship was still strong. In fact, it seemed she loved him more these days. She liked the fact that he turned out to be the bad boy type.

He sighed every time he saw the school building. He thought of playing basketball with Dimitri and Tileyah. He missed it. He even missed Mr. Albright, who would have been extremely disappointed in Kane's new career.

"Yo, we out! Let's go up to Patterson first," Kane said, tired of dealing with pestering crack users. He wanted to hang out with Shyla. He knew they were cutting class today. Keys agreed without hesitation. He didn't like selling drugs anyway. Kane always wondered if he'd last the winter. Keys always talked about rapping instead; and would constantly preach to Kane about quitting. They both seemed to have the talent for it.

"Wait, Wait!" Kane said pulling Keys back as some dude approached, walking in their direction in a hurry. He was alarmed at first, but then Kane recognized the face. He removed his hand from his gun and looked on in delight. "It's my brother!" Kane shouted as a big smile crossed his face. As Craig approached, Kane couldn't help but notice the pointed look on his face.

In an instant, he wrapped two hands around Kane's neck, choking the air from his body. His feet left the ground as his big brother tossed him against the bench. Knocked windless from his landing, Kane sat down to listen to his brother's outburst.

"You're selling drugs in the house where mommy lives!" Craig shouted, barely getting his words out. Keys partially exposed his gun and waited for Kane to give the order. Quickly, Kane shook his head "no" and tried to collect himself. *My brother! How dare he come over here, telling me how to run my life, when I haven't seen him in almost a year*, Kane thought to himself.

After twenty seconds of Craig's tirade, Kane's patience emptied. He pulled out his gun and released the clip, carefully placing it in his pocket. He checked the chamber, ensuring a bullet wasn't present. Craig's eyes widened in disbelief at the exposed gun, and before he could finish his next word, the handle of Kane's gun went flush against the top of his head. The blow could have killed him. Kane blacked out into a violent rage, thinking of everything—the stupid drug users constantly begging for everything, his mother barely showing up at the house, his dropping out of school, his father, and Craig, his brother, leaving him to the streets. If it wasn't for Keys pulling him off his battered sibling, he was sure to have knocked him out—or worse.

Craig laid on the ground, blood dripping from his nose; still in shock from the beating. Their eyes met. Kane saw the pain in Craig's eyes, not from the beating—a deeper pain. Kane said nothing. He was too hurt to express himself verbally. Something he was never good at anyway. He turned and left with Keys to meet up with Shyla at Patterson High.

Days passed.

He hadn't seen his mother since the fight. She was over at Aunt Dorothy's house, disgusted at the site of him. Even his sister didn't bother to check on him; something she did religiously every week. He felt alone—unloved. His family seemed to have turned their backs on him. He heard a knock at the front door. He knew it was Keys with a new package.

"Not tonight," he muttered. He was tired and couldn't bear the thought of sitting on the bench fighting the cold.

He opened the door.

"Yo, Sup? Ready?" Keys was all about business tonight, thinking that the quicker the package was done, the quicker he could go home. Sometimes Kane didn't know why Keys bothered, but then he remembered the reason why. Keys had four sisters and three younger brothers. None of their fathers were around. He had a reason for selling drugs; he had to make money. But Kane had decided to sell because of Nino Brown's character from New Jack City and Shyla, of course. He was lost and he began to realize it.

"Yo, I'm not going today. I'm tired man!" Kane flopped down on the chair in the kitchen.

Keys, smiling, added a quiet smirk. "Well, what are we going to tell Justice!" Keys sat down with a concerned voice. Kane wanted to say he didn't care. He felt like a slave. Countless times they had counted $2,000 a day, but had only received $400 a week. For $400 a week, they had both worked nearly 14 hours a day. It was a rip off. He could have worked full-time at Burger King and make nearly the same.

"I don't know. Tell him I was sick," Kane said in an agitated voice. He really didn't care. Keys sensed his frustration and headed for the living room to turn on the music system. A rap session was just what they both needed. They had rapped together for the past several months, and had written quite a few songs. Their favorite beat to rhyme to was The Symphony beat with Big Daddy Kane, Kool G Rap and Master Ace. Kane watched Keys pull the record from the milk carton. He smiled softly then strolled to the refrigerator in search of an unfinished 40 ounce of Ole English from the night before.

Moments later, music was blasting from Kane's living room as Keys fiddled with the equalizers. They rapped for hours and, for the first time, they recorded the entire night. They performed their duet and then free-styled on instrumental beats like Scenario and one of FU-Schnickens' popular songs. They played back the recordings, listening to them over two fresh 40 ounces of Ole English.

They were shocked at the results.

They were both talented, and for the first time, Kane started to take notice. *Okay,* Kane thought, as he nodded his head in silence. *I'm going to give this a try.* He was in serious thought as the music continued to play in the background. *We could still finish off the drugs at night and blame the delay on a slow night,* Kane plotted, silently. He wasn't quite ready to quit the drug life, but realized that it didn't have a long-term purpose anymore.

Months passed and their sound had developed into something that was well-received by everyone who heard it. They were getting better by the day, and the drug packages were getting more difficult to get through. Justice was frustrated and started to suspect something. Kane's living room became the place to be. The room found itself packed with Shyla's friends and a few others from the building every other night.

His mother would stop by occasionally to pick up some of her clothes, but she would leave so fast he rarely got the chance to see her. However, the dirt-free house impressed her. Shyla spent most of her time there making sure the apartment didn't collect filth. After visiting Justice's apartment, Kane had no problem helping out.

——

Shyla's birthday party was a few days away.

Keys stood in front of the 565 building.

"Yo, ya gotta ask that crack head again why business is so slow," Justice said, frustrated as he handed the package off to Keys. Keys nodded in agreement. Keys and Justice knew each other since they were kids, but Keys had never gotten too close to him. If it weren't for all of his sisters and brothers, he would have stayed in school instead of selling for Justice.

Suddenly Keys' cousin came down the stairs. "Yo, what time is Kay's party again?" He had no idea that Keys didn't want Justice to know about it.

"Kay is throwing a party? I'm there. What time?" Justice asked, smiling. Keys gave him all the details, frowning. They didn't want Justice probing into their drug situation, let alone entertaining him for hours. They had been trying to pull away from Justice for months. They even created a song about how they were being cheated out of money. It was all about rap, dancing, and playing music now.

"Get me another one?" Kane asked, placing the empty bottle of Heineken on the kitchen table. He patted Shyla on her backside as she went to handle his request. Shyla's birthday party finally arrived. She covered the entire place with pink and purple balloons—her two favorite colors. The apartment hadn't been this clean since his father was alive. An honest smile swept across his face as he clutched his pocket, ensuring her birthday gift was still there—an oversized herring-bone chain. Perhaps too loud to wear every day, but he had no doubt she would keep it dangling from her neck anyway. For the first night in weeks, Kane wasn't thinking about his family. Shyla was becoming more of a wife than a girlfriend, and Keys more of a brother than a friend. Things were peaceful.

Keys walked pass the kitchen drinking a Guinness Stout—a more expensive beer. Kane spared no expense—anything for Shyla who was turning out to be quieter than when they first met. She even stopped smoking around him. The apartment was full of people, and although they didn't know for sure if there were troublemakers there, they both agreed not to walk around the house with guns. Their 9mms were carefully stowed away under Kane's mattress.

It was one o'clock in the morning and still no sign of Justice. *Thank God!* Grabbing the drink from Shyla, Kane pulled her into the living room; into the heart of the party. The living room was dark—packed with sweat-filled bodies floating across the room. Gently fighting through the crowd, he finally made his way to the back near the speakers. A soft grin brushed across her face as he gently placed her against the wall.

Suddenly, the music came to an abrupt stop. Everyone paused, giving their attention to Kane. Shyla's face lit up in amazement as the opening to Toney Terry's "When I'm with You" played. The crowd kept silent out of respect. It was their favorite song. Everything was pre-arranged, of course.

He thought about the first time he saw her. He had stayed faithful to her; possibly the only decent thing he'd done all year.

"What's this?" Shyla asked, overjoyed when she noticed the gold-colored jewelry box. She smiled from ear to ear still taken back by the arranged moment.

"It's for you. Happy Birthday. I just want...well...you know, Happy Birthday!" It was Kane's way of saying he loved her. She knew it and broke into tears. As the song finished, she dashed through the crowd with his right hand fixed to hers. They headed for the bedroom, fighting through the small crowd near the hallway.

"Kay," she whispered in a quiet tone, closing the door behind them. Haphazardly, she threw the gift on the side of the dresser without even opening it. "Come here," she said, clutching his black leather belt.

The moment was interrupted by a firm knock on the bedroom door. It was Keys.

"Yo, there're some dudes at the door, said they know Justice." He continued, "But I never saw them before." He waited for Kane's response and stared at the mattress where the guns were stowed. Kane shook his head, "*No.*" He didn't want to get the guns just yet.

He walked out to the living room and opened the peephole.

He was puzzled.

He had never seen them before either. They looked around Kane's age, maybe a bit younger. Their sneakers were a bit worn for them to be drug dealers, but then again, Justice often cheated his workers. Kane eyed one of them and watched them pacing through the peephole. He opened the door a crack.

"Yo, what's up? You letting us in or what?" One guy asked, frustrated. He glared at Kane with wide eyes waiting for an answer.

"Yo," Kane said, "this is my party, and I don't really know ya. Come back with Justice, alright." Kane tried to stay relaxed.

*They're just punks,* he thought to himself.

"Let me up in here," one guy yelled.

A struggle broke out at the front door.

Suddenly, Keys came out of nowhere. "Back the fuck up!" He placed his trusty 9mm right against the intruder's head.

And with a hard shove, Kane sent the guy gliding across the hallway floor then slammed the door. Kane quickly headed back for his gun. He was shocked by how Keys had reacted. He was normally quiet.

Kane's mind was racing, he didn't know what to make of the whole thing. *Would they come back and shoot at the door?* The party crowd was unfazed by the episode. Some of them were from Albany projects and had no problem getting involved, if need be.

"Yo, what's up'? Think we should stop the—" Kane asked.

"Stop the party for those punks? Please!" Keys protested.

Ten minutes later, there was a knock at the front door again.

His nervous habit caused him to pull the gun from his waist. He took a slow walk to look out the peephole. "Its Justice," Kane muttered, a bit relieved, although at this point, they didn't know what was worse: him showing up or dealing with those guys from before.

"Yo, Kay, sup?" Justice asked. His eyes were nearly closed shut from weed; wearing that all too familiar devilish grin, one that Kane and Keys had grown to hate. Two guys followed behind him—they were the same two guys who had caused the commotion moments before.

"It's cool, it's cool," Justice said, still grinning as they all entered the kitchen. The party was unaware of the chill that had crept into the house. Keys leaned against the wall in a restless stare down with one of the guys. Justice looked suspicious; then again, he almost always did. Kane, ready to start shooting at the first sign of trouble, kept his hand close to his waist. At that moment, he knew that this life wasn't for him anymore.

"Yo, Justice. Ya want a drink? We got Heinekens, Budweisers, and I think there's some coolers left." Kane wanted to diffuse some of the tension in the room. It was a good idea. Shyla could get hurt or something worse.

"Yeah, yeah, get me a Heineken," said one of Justice's new workers.

"Yeah, me too," the other imbecile said, as they both headed toward the living room. Keys headed to the back for the beers.

"Yo, Kay, let me holler at you for a minute," Justice asked as he wrapped his arm around Kane's left shoulder.

Just then, Shyla came out of the bathroom and walked pass the two of them.

"Oh, shit!" Justice said as he turned around to drool over the back of Shyla's fitted skirt.

"Yo, that's me," Kane said, reacting sharply to his outburst. Justice continued staring as she walked by, ignoring his plea. Kane's blood went into a hard boil. Barely holding back his rage, he asked, "Yo, Justice, you wanna talk?"

"Damn, she's fine. Shit!" Justice kept up his deliberate rudeness. Kane stopped, turning sharply to knock Justice's arm off his shoulder. The moment grew tense all over again.

Justice turned back to Kane, eyeing him down.

Then he smiled, going back to his grin.

"Yeah, let's talk," he said, shaking off Kane's noticeable anger.

"Yo, Kay, I want you and Keys to show my boys, Majestic and Black, the hustle over here. I want them to take over this spot. I have some new things lined up for ya." Justice looked at Kane seriously as the foolish grin left his face. Kane knew he just wanted those guys to spy on them. He didn't care. He had already decided in the kitchen that he was done hustling.

Kane explained to him that he was getting out of the game and wanted to start rapping full time. Justice listened on, clearly disappointed.

"That's cool; you know you'll always be my little gangster." Justice stood up and headed for the living room.

Keys passed by the bedroom, anxious to hear what had came to light. Kane ran down everything, as Keys' face filled with disbelief. Keys quickly explained how sly Justice could be and that Kane should've thought harder about what to say. Kane didn't care. He'd lost his patience with Justice the moment he disrespected him.

"Get off my arm, please!" Shyla pleaded in the distance. Kane knew Justice was harassing her.

He pulled out his gun then made a dash for the living room.

Keys stopped him.

"Don't. That's what he wants. He wants this. Chill! Let it go." Kane knew he was right. It was uncertain what Justice would have done if he had seen Kane like that. He may have pulled out his gun and started shooting up the party. Keys made sure Kane stayed in the bedroom.

Justice and his new hustlers left soon after the harassment. Despite the presence of Justice, the party was a great success. Most of the crowd had no idea what transpired. Shyla finally opened her gift and rewarded Kane the rest of the night.

They kept their promise and worked with Justice's new workers Majestic and Black. They were a big pain in the ass. Majestic was extra rude to the customers, and Black constantly miscounted money and the drugs. They were idiots. Keys preferred to look out for cops – placing him nearly out of sight from the two of them. Kane, unfortunately, had to deal with their stupidity up close for two weeks. Friday was their last day of hustling. They both explained things to Justice last week. It was all about rapping now.

*Thank God it's over,* Kane thought to himself. *I'm just going to save this $500 until I start working at Burger King or something.*

"I'm done!" Majestic said, handing off the last vial to some old man in yellow, bell-bottom pants from the seventies. They all had a small laugh. It was too funny to resist and, besides, Kane was happy it was pay day.

Justice told them Majestic would handle all the money, which didn't make Kane feel comfortable. But Justice had always been clear on money issues. You'd be as good as dead if you tried messing him over.

"Be right back," Majestic said, leaving. Black followed behind in his over-exaggerated bad-boy walk. Kane thought they both were silly, but they were killers. No question. They were too young and stupid to be scared.

Two hours passed.

Kane and Keys sat on the bench, fighting the chill from the autumn breeze. It was nearly winter, and the last of the leaves were making their way across the stone-covered path.

"Where the hell are they?" Keys asked, looking in both directions.

Two shadows eventually made their way in their direction. One of them was Majestic. Kane had grown used to his voice over the past week and couldn't wait to get away from it.

"Yo, ya got that for us?" Keys asked quickly.

"Yo, Justice said ya didn't do shit, but sit and watch, so he said he would give ya something next week." Majestic tried to hold back a smirk.

"What?" Keys demanded, grinding his teeth in anger.

He jumped up, exasperated and then planted a right hook across the top of Majestic's head. Immediately, Kane's gun left his waist and was pointed straight at Black's forehead. Shocked, Kane stood there, silently awaiting Keys' next move. He watched in disbelief as Keys ripped the new drug package clean from Majestic's pocket. He checked him for a gun and found nothing. It was surprising that they didn't have guns yet. Perhaps Justice thought they were just as stupid as Kane did. All Justice needed was them shooting up everyone to bring heat back to him.

Kane knew now that they had a big problem. They officially had beef with one of the most dangerous drug dealers in the projects. Justice. And these two loose cannons were certain to help with his dirty work.

"Keys!" Kane grabbed Keys off the boy. Majestic laid there on the ground, with his face bloody yet his expression nearly unchanged.

He was crazy.

The next time they crossed paths, it wouldn't be good, but they both weren't prepared to kill them at the moment.

Keys released his hold on Majestic. They both jogged away, heading straight to Justice. Kane couldn't blame Keys for reacting that way. It was inevitable from the moment they started rapping and slipping on sales that Justice would take notice and try to stiff them. He was a business man first, and both Keys and Kane knew how devious he could be.

What now? They really didn't want to exchange gunfire with Justice. Keys lived in the same building as Justice, which was another problem. Glancing over at Keys' worried face as they entered Kane's apartment, Kane could tell that he had begun to regret his reaction.

Three days passed.

There was not a knock at the door or a beep from their beepers. The apartment was quiet and filled with an edginess that kept the both of them pacing back and forth to the living room window. They kept the lights off in an effort to throw Justice off. They sat in the kitchen plotting, running through scenarios with their guns in plain sight.

"Yo, we have to go out. We can't stay like this forever," Keys said, standing in frustration. He was right. They hadn't eaten in nearly two days.

"Let's go to the store around 789," Keys suggested. "We can get some brews and heroes. Maybe even call him from a pay phone to see where his head is at?"

It made sense.

They were both hungry, and it had already been two days and nothing happened. They had at least expected Majestic to knock on the door by now.

They escaped through the back entrance of the building and started their walk to the store. The 789 building was nearly eight blocks away, at the edge of the projects. No one from their side of the projects went to that store. It was too far away; too deserted. The store bordered an oversized parking lot and an abandoned bread factory. No one liked the idea of the place. Too creepy, but it seemed perfect for this situation.

A light drizzle began to fall as they came upon the 24-hour store. The street was layered with wet trash from the rain. Kane stepped over a pile of dog shit. The place was nauseating, nearly causing him to lose his appetite. Despite the repulsive area, they were both happy to be breathing fresh air.

A soft sense of relief was in the air.

They approached the corner store with caution.

Thank God, Kane sighed quietly. It was open, although the doors were securely fastened, leaving them to order behind an oversized fiberglass window.

"Yo, let me get two 40 ounces—" Kane looked around as Keys ran down their order, trying to throw his voice over the barricaded screen.

Suddenly, shadows began to emerge from the darkness.

Kane lowered his eyes for a better look.

# Chapter Six

*Three Years Later in Africa. Northern Angola, a few miles north of Luanda, the capital.*

THE NIGHT FILLED WITH BLACKNESS—a deep dark—lit only by the silence of the moon and distant stars. Kweku looked up, exhausted from the three hundred-mile walk out of the forest. He watched as the palm trees blew across the darkening sky. He, along with his unit had been traveling from the east for weeks and their supplies had grown thin. He thought of his life; the war. He was only nineteen years old, but how long could he hope to live? How many people were left to kill? He struggled to remember his childhood; memories that kept him happy.

They had not eaten in days, and were ordered to meet up with another platoon—if it could be called that. Disorganized bands of children who should have been playing, falling in love and going to school were fighting the war. Most were clueless about what was at stake; however, they all sensed that seizing Luanda and other big southern cities, inside of Huambo and Benguela was the key to victory.

His platoon had not seen much action recently, but had heard gun-fire in the distance on occasion. Their primary objective had been to protect the city of Luanda from the northeast, but when a land mine killed their commander a few weeks ago, they were ordered to regroup on the coast. So much could have gone wrong on such a long journey, but nothing had so far.

They walked with restless legs. Exhausted. Kweku had taken charge of the platoon after their commander died. He had joined the war only a year ago. His uncle, the king of their village, had summoned him and two of his cousins. He ordered them to keep this very platoon away from their village. The platoon was getting too close to the perimeter, it made the king nervous. Sending men out to join the war was originally a successful way to protect the village when the war began. Their job was to persuade nearby platoon commanders not to travel in the village's direction, usually by claiming that the direction was littered with mines and traps. If that strategy did not work, the men would sabotage the platoon's mission or worse. It was not strange to hear that some platoons were fired on by their own men—most likely the work of men from Kweku's village.

All men who left the village were told to return one year after the rainy season, if it was safe to do so. Although, as the war lengthened, men rarely returned. Most were killed, and others, like Kweku and his cousins, were pulled too far away.

He thought of his village constantly and was always thinking, plot-ting of ways to return to his village—home, where dialects of Kim-bundu was the main language, though most of his people spoke several languages, which included Portuguese. Kweku spoke Portuguese well, French, and of course a highly-developed dialect of Kimbundu. His village was untouched by the Portuguese allowing them to retain and further develop Kimbundu.   He learned the languages through his uncle, a brilliant man.  And, although Kweku had an unparalleled flair for hunting, it was his intellect, which earned him the right to marry his younger cousin.  It was something that crossed his mind everyday, even as home drifted farther away with each step.

"Let's stop here," Kweku commanded in Portuguese, spotting a mango tree in the distance.  There were twenty-five men in the platoon and some were older than Kweku, but the commanders liked him most, because he spoke Portuguese the best.  They knew he was educated.  In their eyes, he had been a natural choice for leader.  The men in the platoon walked off into the sand, resting behind a thick line of bushes.  Even at rest, they kept out of plain sight.  Kweku ordered the three youngest soldiers, two thirteen year olds and one fourteen, to fetch mangoes and whatever else could be found.  He demanded they go unarmed; if discovered, the opposition would simply think they were children in search of food.  These decisions kept Kweku in control of the bunch.  He had never fired his weapon, and he had never killed anyone, but the others had.  They compared numbers in amusement nearly every night.

Hours passed.

Bananas, a few mangoes, and the last of some canned rations filled their bellies for the moment.  Most of the men slept, and the rest chatted softly amongst themselves, looking out to the sea.  Kweku took a walk northward along the shore, scoping out the area for tomorrow's journey.  He was told that the next platoon should be in the area.  He walked carelessly, his gun awkwardly strapped around his back.  Had the opposition surprised him, there would not have been time to ready his gun.  He could have been killed easily.

The night grew long. His eyes became heavy. He peeled back an over ripe banana—hoping that eating another one would wake him up. A meal far from the delicious fresh fish dish, Calulu, he was use to eating back in his village. But it had filled his belly, and in this environment, eating was always a blessing.

*There is plenty of food here,* he thought. *There is sure to be company nearby.* He continued his walk, taking in the quiet beauty of the night. The black waters stripped by moonlight. The soft red sand sparkled quietly. Lush palms blew gracefully in the soft winds. Fighting off the mosquitoes, he wondered to himself, *how could a place this beautiful be filled with so much ugliness? This war had carried on for so long, it was difficult to understand what was normal anymore.*

Suddenly, he heard a knocking sound in the distance. Grabbing the gun from his back, he soared into the bushes, struggling to position his rifle just right. He sighed in frustration, upset at how carelessly he kept his weapon. Crouched down, he proceeded with caution as the sound intensified. His eyes widened when he came upon an old two-story stone villa. It looked to have been built around the turn of the century. It sat windowless; cloaked in overgrown bushes and soaring palms.

As Kweku made his way to the back of the villa, he continued to close in on the sound.

It had gotten louder.

Suddenly, he saw a girl's hands fixed against the stone ledge. He made his way around the exposed window for a better look. She was no more than twelve years old. She cried silently. Her small, undeveloped breasts exposed. She hung over the ledge—motionless.

Kweku discovered that the knocking sound came from the soldier's rifle hitting against the stone wall as he made violent strokes into this poor child's body. She was being raped, and from the look on her face,

Kweku sensed that it wasn't her first time. Her face was like stone. Her silent tears seemingly told her story. The drunken soldier continued his brisk motion.

Kweku usually wore a mean face, even back home in his village. People often couldn't tell if he was happy or upset. But this? A coldness like no other crashed upon his face as he clutched his rifle, furious.

The bushes shuddered.

His foot rolled against a small stone.

She looked up.

Their eyes met. He placed his index finger to his mouth, requesting she keep quiet. Fortunately, the soldier didn't hear Kweku. He was too busy enjoying the moment. Kweku crept pass the window and fixed himself against the wall.

Raping a woman in his home village was no light matter. It had been said, the men who dared it were brutally executed, although not before they were tortured for days. A woman is considered the pathway to life and, as such, should be treated with care and love. Kweku boiled in anger as he made his way up the stairs. He was too angry to be nervous. He knew there was a good chance that he would kill this man. Kweku entered the room.

The soldier still relished in the moment.

He crept closer.

Pulling the densely sharpened machete from his left thigh, Kweku swung it with such force that the sound of the wind startled the soldier, causing him to turn quickly.

The knife cleanly pierced through his left shoulder leaving him to crash violently against the stone-covered wall. The battered man tried to recover from the blow as he pulled himself up.

Kweku swung again.

Landing another sharp blow across his head.

The girl, riddled with fear, crawled to a corner and tucked herself in as tightly as possible. With nowhere to run, she looked on in terror.

Blood poured from the man's left temple as he fell to the floor, barely conscious. Kweku had seen a leopard kill his uncle, his father's brother, in the forest, but this was different. He was the killer this time. He took a deep breath and closed his eyes as blood continued to pour from his machete.

A deep calmness passed through his thoughts. He thought of his village and recalled how life was valued there. There were only rumors of men being tortured for extremely horrible deeds, but no one had ever witnessed it. Some said the men were just beaten and told to leave. *But this man*, Kweku thought, *he needed to be killed.* If he let the rapist live, the soldier would surely rape again. Kweku stood over him, trying to think of a good reason to spare the man's life.

He slowly stepped back and positioned the rifle near the man's head.

In an instant, it was over.

One bullet sliced through the front of the man's skull. It was a horrible sight, one Kweku didn't care to examine. He headed towards the girl.

A short distance away, another platoon heard the echoing of Kweku's gunshot.

"What was that?" one soldier asked. In seconds, they all were standing with their rifles pointed in the direction of the villa. "Wait!" The commander yelled, walking in front of the soldier. He leaned forward, listening for another sound. He was a white, Portuguese commander named Commandante João de Sousa. He commanded nearly thousands of soldiers collected from small shanty townships outside of Luanda. He wore a long beard and a noticeable limp from a gunfight two years ago.

His soldiers were mostly kids. There were a few men of age, but most of them should have been in school. Many of them only joined the war to eat and get a rifle. Ever since the city of Luanda fell and was left abandoned, many small towns around the city were looted by gangs and what was left of the local corrupt police. People were unprotected, and so, most joined the army for safety and food.

Commander de Sousa ordered twenty men into flanking positions. Crouched down, they started off in the direction of the villa.

At the villa.

"Are you okay?" Kweku asked gently. The girl was still trembling.

Kweku wondered: *Was there a town nearby? Where did he take her from?* Kweku was anxious and running short on time. Others were sure to come soon.

"Go!" Kweku said, gently helping the girl to her feet. Still puzzled by his kindness, she attempted to cover her breasts. Though her body had been beaten and her t-shirt was dirty and torn, he could see that she was still beautiful.

*She would have made a perfect bride one day,* Kweku thought to himself as she fled down the steps. Lost from her town or village, she was sure to be raped again—or worse. The war spared no woman or child.

Kweku gazed out from the second floor as she disappeared into the forest. *What now,* he wondered, reluctantly heading back to investigate the man's body. He recognized the symbol written on the right shoulder pocket of the uniform. Many soldiers were without uniforms, and the ones that manage one were either well-liked or had been fighting for a long time. Kweku sighed. He had killed someone with rank. He also concluded that he'd killed a soldier from his side. He might have been with the very platoon Kweku had been sent there to meet.

The bushes had begun shuddering from all sides.

Kweku fell against the wall with his rifle fixed to his chest.

*Think, think!* Kweku muttered.

The commander approached the villa, ready to fire.

"Commandante, Commandante!" Kweku shouted to the commander, praying they belonged to the same army. If not, his short life would be coming to a crashing halt.

"Stop!" Sousa shouted, resting the barrel of his rifle on the ground.

"What's your name?" He shouted towards the back door.

"Antonio de Francisco from Commander Fernando's unit," Kweku shouted with a sense of relief. Kweku never used his real name for his own safety. There were many tribes outside his village that didn't get along. In fact, belonging to the wrong tribe sometimes meant instant death. He carried a Latin name outside the village.

He remembered the first time his uncle suggested the name. His cousins had joked about it for weeks. Antonio was an awkward name for him to use, though it fit in some ways. Kweku was tall, lean, very fit, and handsome. Many of the girls in the village had their eyes on him, but it was his cousin Akua whom he loved.

Commander Sousa and his unit slowly headed up the stairs with their guns still drawn. Kweku took a quick glance at the dead rapists and noticed that the fiend was still exposed. He immediately fastened the corpse's pants and placed his gun on the ground. He stood next to the window near the moonlight in plain sight, ensuring he could be seen unarmed.

The commander entered, and Kweku's eyes widened at the white man. The commander demanded an explanation for the dead soldier. Dropping to his knees, he explained that it was a mistake. Kweku claimed that the man did not identify himself and that he thought he was the enemy.

The commander listened as he searched the dead soldier's pockets for anything valuable. The commander gave him a nod. Kweku was spared, although the other soldiers were still puzzled by Kweku's story.

Kweku was still wearing a strange look on his face. It was the first time he'd seen a white soldier, a commander no less. From what his uncle told him, all the white colonialists were driven out of the country. That wasn't true at all. In fact, many of them were knee deep in the war. The commander's face was chiseled with a deep scar. He turned towards Kweku, and ordered him to bring what was left of his unit to the villa immediately. His voice was firm and stern—almost rude. He grabbed Kweku by the arm to reinforce his request.

Three hours later, Kweku's men were assembled at the base camp. He watched in amazement as two war choppers flew overhead. The camp was overflowing with soldiers and commanders. Green tents hugged the shoreline for nearly a mile. It was the main headquarters for the northern army. There were Cuban doctors, professionals, aid workers, engineers, and a breath-taking number of Cuban and Angolan soldiers from different tribes present—including a surprisingly high number of white Angolans. It was more complex than Kweku had imagined.

Kweku followed his unit to their sleeping quarters, but not before taking notice of a stockpile of AK-47s. He tried to remind himself of his uncle's words. *Try to spare life, Kweku. You know our way. Long ago before these men came here and before there were so many tribes, we practiced peace and brotherhood.* He never wanted bloodshed from all sides.

His uncle was wiser than many of the elders from the village. He was educated in Luanda, and had traveled deep into the deserts of Namibia all the way up to the coast of Gabon a few years before the height of the conflict. He became king when Kweku's father died a few years ago.

Kweku's uncle implored him to have patience and understanding, but the war grew too complicated. It became harder and harder to heed his uncle's words. It became about survival—nothing more.

Finally, Kweku entered his tent.

*Sleep!* He flopped down on the sand. Within moments, the night's sky whitened as the sun expanded over the horizon. Though it was daytime, Kweku planned to take as much sleep as he could. He had been walking for weeks and only managed three hours of sleep a day. The forest had been crawling with wildlife, keeping his slumber short.

Kweku thought of the man he killed, but the memory was too horrible to dwell on. Instead, he tried to remember his village back home.

His home rested between two majestic mountains, high as the eye could see. His uncle often told stories of the mountains, claiming that the top only had eyes for God himself. There was a lake there—a large lake filled with blue water. It came from a great river that flowed northward through the country. It traveled beneath the mountains to form a body of fresh water so breath taking, that when it was seen for the first time, its beauty could not be placed into words. Only a lasting pause would do.

A bit of a fairy tale.

But, his village was real. As real as the lush grass and palm trees that graced its border.

.

The huts were each carefully constructed, made of rich red mud with firmly-placed branches on top of them. There were several huts, some slightly larger than others, because of royalty and family size. The village had everything it needed.

There were only two ways to enter. A dense, dark, and mysterious passageway existed at the bottom of the mountains, which kept the place untouched by humans until their ancestors had discovered it thousands of years before Africa was given borders.

The other entrance was a narrow passage south through the dense forest. A forest filled with wild beasts, leopards and snakes. They managed to fence the area off in an attempt to protect the village, but there had been many deaths by animals over the centuries. The most recent one had been Kweku's Uncle Bongani. He had been at the well getting water for supper when a leopard had sprung out of the blackness. It snapped his neck instantly. Kweku and Akua, his daughter, watched motionless as the leopard dragged his lifeless body into the deep, misty forest. The king claimed that the death was a sign from God and demanded that his life not be mourned.

The King had said:

*"This man has served us well. It is the will of our fathers. We wait in patience for the winds, my brothers and sisters. There we will find him well."*

His words were short and quick, but the meaning, implied so much more. In the village it was believed that their ancestors from the dawn of time had summoned a supernatural wind that carried spirits of the dead to the spirit world—souls that walked the earth as heroes and as true followers of both love and brotherhood. The wind traveled through the village each year with only a few earning passage.

—

Akua, Bongani's first daughter, struggled not to mourn his death. She would cry in her sleep, tucked away in the corner. Many from the village knew she would soon be the princess, so they comforted her with gifts and numerous folktales. Kweku would sneak her off to the forbidden place, as much as time permitted.

A backdrop of a natural spring from the mountains created a warm endless flow of fresh water. The waterfall was so erotic that children were not permitted to go there. Only lovers and the married were allowed.

They'd sneak out in the dead of night and duck behind the bushes to watch lovers mate.

—

Once a woman, muttering words in Kimbundu was suddenly stopped by her own passion—the tongue of the past spoken sharply with each breath as she had whimpered into her lovers' ear. The enclosed waterfall surrendered to the dark of the night, though moonlight managed to stretched through its' open spaces. It left behind the shadows of their bodies. Kweku and Akua watched with keen eyes and listened with sharp ears.

The woman's body was held beneath the running water, as the man clutched the back of her head with force. His shoulders, broad, lean with muscles protruding from his back. She grabbed the back of his head as he raised her from the ground, pressing her against the stone-covered wall.

The water crashed against their bodies like a violent wave. Their silhouette crossed the moonlight, exposing her breast and the back end of his arm. Their skin was rich, black-smooth like silk. She moaned in pain. Another touch of moonlight exposed his back, this time thrusting. A hint of blood trickled down from her ankle; her skin had broken from the sharp, rocky edge. Her cut went unnoticed as she continued to moan from his strokes.

—

This would occur nearly every night. Even during the rainy season when the waters were the heaviest, they would still find lovers twisting in the ambiance of this place. Kweku always dreamt of making love to Akua there on her eighteenth birthday, but for now he only had his daydreams and this dreadful war with no end in sight.

"Antonio, wake up!" The commander kicked the bottom of Kweku's worn out boots. "Come here!" The commander flipped the tent back down as Kweku quickly collected his things. The sun scorched his head instantly as he crawled out of the tent. It was still daylight. Kweku had never felt this type of heat. He had lived around the mountains where the air was fresh and cool. He tagged along behind the fast-walking commander, wiping his mouth in thirst. He'd only gotten four hours of sleep.

"You will remain commander of your unit." The commander tapped on Kweku's left shoulder, delighted to bestow the honor. Kweku smiled, although he could care less. He just wanted to return home.

He looked on in amazement as they entered the commander's tent. The tent was larger than the rest. It was the situation room where the strategies were planned. There seemed to be people of all races inside:

Cubans, mulattos, white Portuguese, and some Black Angolans from the outer cities.

Kweku was carefully placed in the back as the commander made his way to a closer seat. They talked strategy while Kweku listened carefully in silence.

"The south of the country is holding steady, but I think we will need more forces to secure the following check points along the front. The South African army is trying to use the north coast of Namibia to get supplies in. They want us to set up a stronger perimeter south of Luanda. And, as for the armies protecting the south and east of the city, they have lost six check points in several towns. In Benguela, there is the most trouble. We need reinforcements there as soon as possible. We lost that city two weeks ago. In the north, we have to send more reinforcement," the general explained. This top Portuguese general seemed extremely knowledgeable about the entire situation. Kweku listened as the general continued on in detail about the northern platoons.

*All these different cities and places*, Kweku thought to himself, as he fell into another daydream. *All these innocent people caught in the crossfire.* He could just imagine the devastation. His uncle told him that the war had been going on for at least ten years and there was still no end in sight. *What is it inside these men that gives them the will to fight this long*, Kweku thought to himself.

As the commanders continued to talk, he slowly began remembering his uncle's words again.

*"It's the weakness in these men that brought this place into ruin. God has left the souls of those who chose not to live in harmony with the Earth and, instead, have chosen to live for themselves. As for the innocent victims*

*who have felt their wrath, they will be carried into the winds from the north—the wind of our fathers."*

Kweku deeply believed in what his uncle and the other village elders had told him. It must be true. The country was growing empty and the native Angolans were dying the most. He drew the line at killing the innocent and tribe loyalty was irrelevant to him.

His uncle would speak of these times with sadness and anger. He would say these men had created an idea that crippled the planet simply to please themselves. He often said that dominance over all other living things came with great responsibility—one that had been granted to us by God. But we had failed, and would surely reap the consequences. He spoke of a reckoning far deeper and greater than the war Kweku was faced with now.

The ongoing war also meant the village was now in danger of being discovered. The elders claimed the place was protected, but when the villagers heard sounds of gunfire in short distances, the king and elders decided to send men out to provide extra security. Of the first group he sent, only fifteen had returned out of seventy. The number of men in the village was diminishing. There was a time when the village had nearly four hundred souls, and now the number was down to nearly a hundred.

The village remained a place for brotherhood. It was beautiful. Kweku's grandfather said it was heaven on earth, a sacred place—God's place.

Kweku came abruptly out of his daydream.

"Do you understand everything?" Commander Sousa asked, standing in front of Kweku with a concerned look as the meeting ended. Kweku nodded his head in agreement. His orders were simple. He was to take his men, plus an additional twenty of Sousa's men back east, almost to where they were stationed before. Next, they were to press northward a half mile each day. It seemed like a death trap. The idea was to press north until they ran into resistance. This would give headquarters some idea of hostile positions.

If Kweku's unit was discovered, there would be a battle and there were sure to be casualties. Kweku understood this, but he had already begun his plan to abandon his unit and head for home with his cousins. He wondered if he would get his chance before the conflict.

# Chapter Seven

T HE DAY PASSED.

Most of Kweku's unit chatted about the Jeeps and the helicopters, which constantly flew overhead. Kweku had not met anyone in the unit he liked. Many of them were too young to care about why their lives had been put in harm's way. It was just another wartime tragedy. His two cousins, Kgosi and Kirabo, kept quiet, like Kweku insisted. A year had passed, but they were still in shock since leaving the village. Kweku always protected them. Kgosi was next in line to be King, but his father had no choice but to send him too. They were the oldest of the king's children. Kgosi was sixteen and Kirabo thirteen.

Kweku's unit would be heading out in two days. He thought that since he was heading back east, there was a chance he could escape with his cousins and head for home. He knew this war was no place for them. Night fell as Kweku made a fire near the tent. He ordered his group to gather around. They all knew he was still commanding the unit; they had seen him shaking hands earlier with Commander Sousa as he entered the command station.

"Okay," Kweku began talking over the two soldiers still chatting as they made their way to the fire. Kweku explained their next mission, making them aware that they would be traveling straight east into the forest and would not head south around the perimeter of Luanda. He wanted to avoid a possible gun fight with any gangs or ex-police groups. The war had left the capital, Luanda, a ghost town. The white Portuguese colonists that once populated much of the city seemed to flee the city overnight.

Many escaped to Brazil just across the Atlantic Ocean, and some had fled back to Portugal. During their rule most of the Africans lived outside of the city. This was not by choice, but due to an appalling system that was put in place before the war. It was a horrible system; one that Angolans were determined to change by force—and they did.

Although, it seemed that once the government haphazardly surrendered control back to the people, it spelled disaster for Angola. There was no leadership, no concrete plan for the future. And so came the race for control over the country's resources. The white-controlled South African army began to converge on Angola from the south with an interest in oil, but more concerned with riverbanks for hydro-electronic power. Another group of Africans began to converge into the cities from the great desserts of Namibia to the west, collaborating with the South African government. To complicate the situation even further, Africans from the north—in the Congo region—decided to join in on the mayhem. And then there was the force that Kweku had joined, which was trying to keep all of the other forces from breeching and seizing major cities like Luanda, which were under their control. All the different groups considered the other groups to be their enemies. All the while, it was the people of Angola absorbing the bullets and stepping onto landmines. A tragedy that seemed to last forever.

The war brought out the worst in humanity and Africans had been suffering and dying because of it for decades.

The war had destroyed the brotherhood of men, encouraged weakness, and destroyed the one idea that had been carried forward by all tribes since the beginning. Love. Kweku's people kept to these old ways. They had done so long before countries had borders and tribes lived with names.

The soldiers sat around the fire as Kweku described the strategy.

"Antonio!" Commander Sousa shouted, arriving with an additional twenty men. Kweku had come across some of the same men at the villa the night before.

"This is Amandio," Commander Sousa said, pointing to an odd-looking soldier. Amandio was a few years older—shorter than Kweku. Kweku clearly remembered him from the villa—the deep scar that creased his right eye was hard to forget. His right eye, when opened wide, shone pearly white. It was truly frightening at night, although Kweku had been trained in the village to control such fears. Amandio had been the first soldier up the stairs after the commander the night of the incident in the villa. The soldier that Kweku had killed had been Amandio's best friend. They had come from the same town, just south of Luanda.

Commander Sousa explained that Amandio was his second in command and would take over command if he were injured. They used the word "injured" around the foot soldiers because so many of them were too young or inexperienced to absorb the true meaning of the word which meant death. Amandio glanced at Kweku several times, as the commander finished explaining the mission called "Mission Green." Kweku caught Amandio gazing at him several times.

*This guy is going to give me trouble*, Kweku thought to himself.

Most of Kweku's soldiers were already mingling with the new troops from Sousa's group. Some were even from the same towns. Kweku and his cousins stood out from the bunch. They looked new, teeth as white as snow, darker skin, smooth like silk; and were taller and more fit than the rest. The soldiers talked for a few hours then fell off to sleep. Kweku and Amandio said nothing to each other. They just continued stealing glances at each other.

Meanwhile, back at the village.

It was three weeks before the rainy season. The village was already preparing for the heavy rain by preserving fruits, vegetables, and fish. Their huts designed to withstand the storm, would protect the food for the vigorous four months. They were made of thick tree bark and a thick red mud, which seemed nearly impenetrable to the rain. But, before the rain would come there were the winds; winds so strong, even the strongest palm trees would nearly bend to the ground. Amazingly, the huts year after year would survive with minimum damage.

Despite the staggering storm, it was a special time. The village partied for weeks before sending off the dead. They'd paint themselves in white stripes with soft clay. It remained on their bodies for weeks. The women would shake the earth with their feet, as the men rugged hands pummeled their makeshift drums. The rest watched and sang in complete harmony.

It was the most celebrated time of year.

A sacred time.

Even the soldiers at war, could not escape the power of the storm. The fighting was always known to taper off a bit and, as for the village, it usually brought a few months of safety.

"Akua, he will return," the king said, gently placing his hand upon her shoulder as she looked out into the jungle. Kweku had been gone for over a year. He should have returned months ago. *Would he end up like the others,* she thought.

Akua loved him. Her eighteenth birthday had passed months ago, leaving many men of the village anxious. They admired her. Her voice was soft, but her words, smart and straight. And her beauty, it was unimaginable.

Her face rich and smooth. Her skin dark and even. But, it was her eyes that Kweku loved most, they were bright like the northern star and clear like the fresh water that circled the village. She stood tall, slender, and carried a figure so alluring; it held captive the imagination of nearly every man in the village. But it was Kweku whom she loved. Their handsomeness combined was to make the perfect unit. She thought of the waterfall more so now than before. It was not forbidden for her anymore. She was of age, ready to marry.

"I know," she said calmly as she turned away from the jungle. It was nearly nightfall and the dancing had already started around the fires. The time of the great winds were near. She could hear faint songs a short distance away.

It grew louder, in perfect rhythm.

A beautiful sound.

*It was the voices from God,* Kweku's father would say.

Back at base camp, off the coast, miles from Luanda; Kweku's unit now made up of thirty-six men, packaged rations and re-armed themselves. They gathered around Kweku's tent. Clouds covered the sky, and the fierce winds began filling the air with sand.

"Let's go, let's go!" Commander Sousa shouted from the back of the truck with a wave of his hand. They were hitching a ride south for a few miles down along the coast before heading east into the forest. Kweku grabbed his gun and ordered the men into the truck. Amandio watched him in the distance as he grabbed the command radio and followed behind the others.

Three hours passed.

The winds died down a bit.

Finally, the truck stopped in the sand.

The men fell in line off the truck—some with uniforms, some not; some short, some tall; most of them were too young to be there. The commander wished them luck as the truck drove up the coast, leaving a fresh tire track in the sand.

# Chapter Eight

WEEKS PASSED.

Kweku and his unit were a long way from the coast—nearing the heart of the forest.

Loud coughing came from the back of the line. Kweku turned just in time to see Kirabo, his younger cousin, flop down against the base of a tree. The thirteen-year old was sweating profusely. Kweku quickly headed over.

"Stop!" Kweku ordered. His sharp request echoed up and down the line as they all finally came to a stop.

*God, he was bitten,* Kweku muttered. He worried in silence, keeping his emotions in check. They'd been walking for weeks and, with the heavy rain, animals were sure to be out in the forest, especially snakes.

"What happened?" Amandio demanded, bursting from the front of the line in frustration. The unit had stopped in an open area, not a smart place to rest. "We must get to the river! Now!" Amandio ordered, ignoring Kirabo.

"Wait!" Kweku yelled, looking up at Amandio. It was a tense moment for the unit; everyone carefully focused on each word from the both of them. If Kweku showed any weakness, they were sure to lose respect for him.

"No, we leave now!" Amandio said. He turned and headed off to the front.

Sudden gunfire discharged.

It was Kweku.

The bullet nearly hit Amandio's back foot. The entire unit was startled. They jumped back anxious, except for Amandio. He turned with a nervous smile then clenched his rifle. Kweku took notice and took aim at the middle of his head, ready to fire.

Amandio stood there eying Kweku, testing him.

Seconds later, Amandio, wisely relaxed his rifle in amusement.

The unit was shocked by Kweku's actions. Most of them had not seen him ever discharge his weapon. They always silently questioned his nerve. And although most of them had discharged their weapons, it had been from afar—often killing women and children, even babies were caught in the crossfire. They shot blindly from a distance, during long-range combat—hardly something to brag about.

Now, it was clear who was in charge.

Kweku would have killed him.

Amandio knew it.

Kweku turned back to help his cousin. *Firing the gun was a mistake.* He could have easily given away their position. Kirabo looked famished. Kweku looked on as blood trickled from his mouth with each cough.

Kweku knew that anyone who got sick in the forest was likely to die. He looked at his younger cousin then grinded his teeth. They were too far out to turn back to the base camp, but Kweku still radioed in. Commander Sousa was fighting far south of them, in northern Lobito.

Kweku spoke with a doctor from headquarters who told him to give his ailing cousin plenty of water. Kweku could not help but smirk in disbelief. *They don't care about any of us,* Kweku thought as he lifted Kirabo over his back in one motion. Kweku's strength prevailed, even after weeks of walking and fighting the rain. He moved with an unfaltering steadiness that amazed the others. They wondered constantly about where he had come from. They continued walking northward another ten miles. Kweku carried Kirabo the entire time.

Night fell.

They finally came to the river. Kweku looked down on the black water from the forty-foot cliff, exhausted. They would sleep there for the night and set up camp tomorrow.

Still thinking of home, Kweku looked around, trying to locate something familiar. But he was still too far away. He knew that if he traveled far enough East he was sure to see something familiar. As Kirabo worsened, his thoughts of an escape grew larger. *But how?*

The heat of the sun woke him, as Kweku threw a shirt over his face. It was finally morning.

"Commander, commander!" a young soldier anxiously pulled at Kweku's shoulder and pointed down at the river. The commotion slowly began to wake the others. Kweku looked down at the river and had to use every ounce of strength to avoid showing emotion. He took a deep breath and gazed at the bodies below that soaked the water red with blood. Men, women, and children, hundreds of them floated lifelessly. They had been butchered. The entire unit looked on in silence. Even Amandio stood there quietly. It seemed to be a dumping ground for the dead, but these were not soldiers—they were villagers. Kweku thought of his home and decided right then that the first chance he had, he was going to escape with his cousins.

"We should—," a soldier stopped, unable to finish the words as a bullet from afar tore through his chest. He was no more than twelve or thirteen. In an instant his lifeless body violently crashed against a tree.

They had been discovered!

More shots were fired in the distance.

"Get back! Get back!" Kweku shouted, as he collected Kirabo and retreated a safe distance away from the cliff.

The opposing army appeared out of the bushes and headed straight for them. There were over two hundred men, out numbering them six to one.

The gunfire continued.

In seconds, it intensified as more of Kweku's soldiers were killed.

It was a slaughter—Kweku's unit was overwhelmed.

Then, a loud, thunderous sound vibrated through the forest.

It was Kweku.

He had inched closer by the overhang and started to return fire. Amandio a few feet away followed soon after. They were at the front line, at close range—true soldiers, both of them. It was brave. It was easier to run.

The unit was down to seven men. Some ran without looking back and the rest were dead, riddled with bullets.

But Kweku continued shooting.

He sighed as one of his bullets caught an enemy soldier in the forehead. The guy could not have been older than his younger brother—ten or eleven.

In the face of such fierce return fire, the opposition below began to take cover. What was left of Kweku's unit now had an advantage over the opposition. They were in an elevated position and hit nearly every target in site.

The shooting continued—gunfire filled the air with smoke.

Moments later, nearly fifty of the two hundred opposing soldiers lay dead along the river. It was a nasty battle.

The shots finally came to a crawl and for the moment the enemy was unable to advance from below. Kweku, his cousin Kgosi, and a few loyal to Amandio did their work well. In their courageous stand, they kept the enemy at bay, giving them time to escape. The winds had picked up, it was sure to rain soon. They all agreed to make a run for it then. It was quiet, but the danger was still there lurking.

Finally, the rain began to fall.

Kweku turned to look for Kirabo and found Kgosi, his other cousin, standing over Kirabo's lifeless body.

Kweku watched as blood dripped from Kgosi's hand. It was still tightly wrapped around the trigger of his rifle. A bullet had cut him across the wrist, nothing major.

Kgosi paid no attention to the open slash. His face was hollow, detached. He caught Kweku's eye. He looked as if he'd matured a whole twenty years. *It's time to go home,* Kweku thought, turning his back to hold in his emotions. It would surely cloud his judgment.

Kgosi looked down at his younger brother with a heartbreaking stare. He knew there wasn't enough time to bury him. Leaving the dead unburied went against the core principles of their beliefs, and Kgosi was a strong believer.

As the rain thickened, the unit gathered quickly to plan their escape. The enemy thought there were hundreds of soldiers on the cliff, but there were only seven. Kweku knew their great stand off wouldn't last. It was only a matter of time before the other army would close in on their position. They needed to escape.

The plan was simple: let off several rounds and then run back west to headquarters. The radio had been damaged during the fighting, but Amandio was convinced it could be fixed. He attached it to his waist and then grabbed a bag of rations off a dead soldier.

Kweku was still plotting his escape back home, but his ammunition was running thin and those loyal to Amandio were holding most of the bullets now.

Many miles away at the village.

The rain pounded the sturdy mud huts. The wells overflowed with water. No one dared to go outside. They were content to stay tucked inside, peacefully listening to old tales from the elders.

Back at the battlefield.

They released a round of shots from the top of the cliff. Kweku wisely shot less; he knew Amandio would not give him more ammunition.

They all turned and sprinted towards the thickest part of the forest, fighting through the heavy rain. It was a great time to escape. He paused looking for Kgosi. Nothing. Finally, he spotted him next to Amandio. His plan was spoiled. He had no time to regret it. He continued running with the group.

Weeks passed.

The rain was endless.

Tired and hungry, they stopped to rest. They had run out of food days ago, and Amandio had been growing more and more agitated. It spelled trouble for Kweku and Kgosi. Moments after they had run from the river, Amandio had disarmed Kweku by threatening Kgosi's life. They were his hostages now. Kweku knew he had no intention of keeping them alive. They were just his amusement now.

"Antonio, mangoes! Look, there! Go get them!" Amandio ordered, smirking as he used the name Antonio. He suspected that Kweku was lying about his name.

Kweku pulled Kgosi with him but Amandio stopped them both. "No, he stays," Amandio barked, then leaned in towards Kgosi and asked, "What's your real name?"

Kgosi answered with a straight face, "Alberto." Kgosi always answered his questions cleanly. They had memorized their new identities for weeks before they left the village.

"You are from Catete? Where in Catete?" Amandio demanded. He pulled his rifle from his back. If Kgosi answered incorrectly, there was no telling what Amandio would do. The situation was so fragile.

"Amandio! Here is your fruit," Kweku said, interrupting the interrogation.

He snatched the fruit from Kweku's hand and continued questioning them. Kweku answered and saved his cousin's life. *But for how long?* Kweku knew they had to make a move to escape soon or they would be dead within a day, perhaps hours.

The mango tree was soaked from the rain. The sun rose high into the sky.

It was morning.

*Finally*, Kweku thought. Mosquitoes near the fruit plant could be deadly at night. In fact, a mosquito may have been what killed Kirabo. It seemed the rain brought out every insect in Angola. It was so difficult to rest. Kweku and Kgosi, ignored for the moment, relaxed against the tree as Amandio and his followers devoured the mangoes. They rested for a few hours then continued west. Amandio knew the shore was only a few miles away. He could smell a hint of salt water.

Kweku did not have time to explain his entire plan of escape to his cousin, but told him that when he saw him run, he should run too. It was a reckless plan, but he was desperate. He didn't believe Amandio would keep them alive for much longer.

Amandio had carelessly left the both of them in the back as they headed for the shore. Kweku looked back constantly, seeking a good direction to run. He tapped Kgosi and nodded his head, signaling that it was nearly time.

He found an opening to run and he grabbed Kgosi by the arm.

They turned back; ready to make a dash for it.

But then, a loud rugged voice filled the air.

It was Amandio. "Why are they in the back? In front, now!" He pulled at Kgosi's arm, tugging him along. Kweku followed. His plan to escape was lost again. He closed his eyes heartbroken. There was no opportunity to escape at the front. He would have to kill Amandio and his men to escape now, and without a weapon, his chances of survival were grim. Kweku walked forward over the fallen branches that broke off from the heavy winds. It reminded him of his village. He put his head down and thought of home.

Hours later.

"Look, look!" Yelled one of Amandio's soldiers. Kweku noticed traces of red sand a few minutes ago, but did not care to mention that they finally had reached the shoreline.

"What is that over there?" Shouted one of Amandio's men. *He notices everything. He'd be the first one to notice our disappearance if we tried another escape,* Kweku thought to himself.

They walked forward towards the shoreline.

And, there it was.

A body laying on the sand, barely ashore.

They watched in disbelief as it continued struggling out of the water. As they moved closer, the situation became even more bizarre. They looked at each other in total shock, silenced by what they saw. Even Kweku and his cousin looked on in amazement.

# Chapter Nine

THREE YEARS BEFORE in Brooklyn near the corner store.

A dark shadow moved out of the darkness. Kane strained his eyes for a better look. Three men emerged. Kane tapped Keys' shoulder anxiously. "Yo, we gotta go, man!"

Suddenly, gunfire erupted.

It came from that direction.

"Motherfucker!" A voice shouted in the distance.

It was Majestic.

They had been followed. Kane reached for his gun. Nothing. He left it on the kitchen table. They ducked down and headed for the old bread factory next door. More shots exploded against the store's protected glass window. Some hit the base of a tree, inches away from Kane's foot.

Keys knew Majestic would not stop until the police came or the both of them were dead. Justice was certainly behind it or with him, although at the moment, it was too dark to tell.

Keys kicked in the side door of the bread factory. They ran through, trying to keep quiet. The place was dark, dusty and filled with rats. Keys carefully jumped over the tin barrel and headed up to the second floor. Kane followed him closely. Kane could hear his heartbeat pounding against his chest. *How were they going to get out of this?*

They approached the second floor.

It was nearly empty with no place for them to hide.

Suddenly, a loud bang came from the first floor.

It was Majestic.

He kicked in the side door.

They crept to the back near the stairwell where it was the darkest. Much of the second floor was lit by the street light. They both sighed, disappointed to find that the back door had a five-inch thick chain wrapped around the knob. They would never be able to open it. It would take a shot from Keys' gun to break it free, but the sound from the discharge would certainly reveal their location.

They fixed themselves behind a column next to the door where they could listen to the commotion coming from the first floor. *Maybe they'll leave,* Kane thought to himself. They anxiously pressed their backs to the wall, trying to stay out of sight.

Just then.

"We know you're in here, motherfucker!" Majestic shouted from the first floor.

"Shut the fuck up, stupid," said a deeper voice. It sounded like Justice. Kane's heart dropped. He took a deep breath to calm his already spiraling nerves. He looked at the stairwell door again. He was hoping Keys was thinking the same thing. *We have to fire the shot to break the lock.* They were sitting ducks if they stayed.

"Yo, the second floor!" Justice said, trying to soften his voice. When they heard the sound of sneakers on the steps, they knew Justice and the others were headed in their direction. They had to make a move. Kane turned quickly and looked at Keys.

He stared at the door.

They had no choice.

Keys agreed and cocked the gun back, aiming carefully.

A deafening shot echoed throughout the factory. It was earsplitting, especially in the enclosed space. Kane clutched his ears. The bullet clipped the chain, but the lock held. It was still fixed across the door.

Justice and his two-man crew sprung to the second floor. Keys heard the loud sneakers racing up the stairs. Hysterical, he shot again—this time clearing the lock from the door.

In an instant, a barrage of gunfire traveled in their direction. Two shots hit Keys on the left side of his waist and another hit him down by his ankle. He was forced back behind the column. Amazingly, Kane went untouched. He dove into the stairwell. Keys was trapped—cornered—with bullets lodged into his left side.

Kane held the door open, still in shock from the gunfire. He urged Keys to launch himself over, but it was too risky.

"Yo, you alright, man?" Justice asked, sarcastically. He shot again and hit the corner of the door. Kane jumped back frantically, but kept his hands fixed at the door. He waited, courageously, for Keys' next move.

"Kay...Kay," Keys said, looking up—fighting the pain. Blood pooled beneath him as he tried to sit himself upright. "Kay. Here...take it!" Keys slid his gun across to Kane. "Go. Go, Kay," he instructed, then paused, "Make that record," he added and tried to crack a smile through the pain.

Kane stood there motionless, listening to Keys' farewell. Still stunned, Kane stood by the door, shaking his head. Then more shots rang out, striking the column again.

"Go, Kay! It's okay," Keys pleaded with Kane to leave. They eyed each other as the stairwell door slowly closed. Kane sprinted down the stairs, listening to Keys shout threats as if he was still armed—trying to buy Kane more time.

"Yeah, come this way if you want! I know it's you Justice."

Kane kicked the front door open and headed down the back streets at top speed. He stopped near a Dunkin Donuts beneath the subway. He gently opened the door, concealing the bloody gun then headed towards the counter, trying to catch his breath.

He wiped the blood from his hand.

"Hi," he said to the Korean girl behind the counter. "Excuse me, do you have a bathroom?" He hoped she wouldn't ask him to purchase something first. Keys had all his money. She pointed to the left as she passed him the key. He slammed the door shut and flopped onto the toilet seat, his thoughts racing.

*How could I leave him?*

*How could I?*

He sighed and threw his fist against the cream-colored wall. He pulled the gun from his waist, grabbed the knob to the door, and then released it. He considered going back for Keys, but then paced around frantically. His emotions were out of control.

—

Meanwhile, back at the bread factory.

"Yo, man, you alright?" Justice asked, amusing himself again. He tucked away all the years he knew Keys. They had lived in the same building for years and were never short on playing "Follow the leader" together when they were younger. Yet it came very easy for Justice to ignore their history.

Keys remained silent as he watched his blood thicken. It ran across the stairwell, heading down the steps. His pants were soaked red. He could feel a faint chill run through his body. He was dying. Justice's 357 magnum had torn a gruesome hole through his left side.

Suddenly more gunfire.

Two shots hit the back wall and then the column again. Justice had begun to inch closer after Keys did not return fire. He continued to taunt, but Keys was too weak to respond. Justice inched closer. Before long, they all arrived at the column. Justice, Majestic and Black. They took notice of Keys' left hand. It was soaking in a pool of blood. His own. Justice slowly turned into full view of Keys with the barrel of his gun pointing down at his forehead.

"Let me?" Majestic offered, jumping in front of Justice, waving his gun foolishly. *They were all fools.*

"Get the fuck—!" Justice scolded. "Wait downstairs," he said in disgust. Then a memory flashed back. He remembered laughing and shooting dice with Keys in The Hole a few weeks ago. He sighed.

"Kev?" Justice said, calling Keys by his real name. Keys looked up at him, sweating. Too weak to hold his head, he simply dropped it back down to face the floor.

Justice lifted his gun again.

The second floor was frozen quiet.

Then the inevitable happened.

The bullet cut through Keys' left temple as his upper body slid lifelessly down the column. He killed him, in cold blood.

—

In the bathroom at Dunkin Donuts.

Kane paused to look at the mirror over the sink. He stared at himself, calming down a bit. "Keys is dead. I know it," he said calmly, sighing. He began to think a bit clearer. *What now?* Justice and his crew would kill him on sight. He could never go home or to Shyla's house. It would be too risky.

"Jade," Kane blurted out, relieved.

His sister.

Although Jade had her own problems with her boyfriend, Trevor, she would let Kane stay with her until he figured things out. He couldn't count on Craig after their fight. Jade was his only option. She lived up in the Bronx. It was far enough out of Brooklyn to feel protected.

# Chapter Ten

"WHEN YOU'RE DONE WITH THE PEAS, go see Jose in aisle two," Frost, the night manager, shouted down the aisle at Kane. It had been seven months since Keys' murder. Jade had taken him in with two conditions: he had to work and he had to get his GED the following year.

Justice and most of his crew has been arrested and charged with Keys' murder. The owner of the nearby shop got a good look at Black's face. The cops eventually got what they needed to pin the murder on Justice and Majestic.

Even with Justice gone, Kane had no interest in returning to Brooklyn any time soon. Justice had many friends and, with the trial still going on, it was best to stay out of sight. He spent his time working in a supermarket blocks away from his sister's apartment and writing music.

Kane and Shyla talked on the phone, mostly. She came over a few times, but thought the ride to the Bronx was too far. She hated the Bronx. Last month on his eighteenth birthday, they went out for a movie near Gun Hill Road. She complained the entire time. Their relationship had deteriorated. After Keys' death, Kane became more consumed with writing.

Jade's apartment was small, a one-bedroom. To make matters worst, he was forced to listen to Jade and her boyfriend, Trevor, argue for hours on end. Trevor was a wanna be gangster who sold dope around the corner from the apartment. He hung out with a Puerto Rican dude named Manuel; they called him Manny for short. Kane kept Keys' gun to be reminded of that dreadful night, though he never kept it loaded. He was done with that life. He was saving money, writing, rapping every chance he could and although Shyla would listen through the phone, it was the stock boys at the supermarket that got the ear full.

"Cool," Kane shouted over the music playing through his headphones, in response to Frost's request. It was nearly time for the market to close. When Frost closed up, he allowed nearly everything—except stealing. He was an albino whom everyone called Frost. He didn't mind. It was an innocent tease to a person that was well-liked throughout the store. Everyone treated him the same and he loved them for it, but it was Kane he liked most.

"Come back this way—" Kane said, rhyming over a Das EFX song. He continued on, remembering his rap sessions with Keys in his living room back in Brooklyn. His voice was thunderous and getting louder by the second. Two girls at the corner of the aisle stopped to listen. Unaware of the building crowd, now coming from both sides of the aisle, he continued his steady stream of lyrics as he stacked the Del Monte peas on the shelf. He sounded amazing. His voice was naturally deep and rugged, unlike the typical rapper. He sounded like a seasoned professional.

"Yo, Kay!" Patrick, a co-worker who worked in the dairy section, tried to warn him through the loud volume on his walkman. Startled, he jumped back against the shelf as a few cans rolled across the floor. Patrick smiled and shook his head. Kane gave up a soft grin, embarrassed.

As the crowd departed, one man remained, eyes still fixed on Kane in amazement. "Excuse me," the older gentleman said, as he approached. "Do you just rhyme for fun?" He smiled, still amazed.

"Yeah, just playing around," Kane said as he continued collecting the fallen cans from the floor.

"Well, how 'bout you come down to Fresco's Bar and Grill. It's in Manhattan. Let me give you the directions." The man pulled out a piece of paper to write on.

"Nah, what's this? I just be joking around." Kane squirmed, unaware of his talent. He curled up in shyness as the man continued.

"Listen, my name is Larry Brown. People just call me LB," the old man said as he leaned against the shelf of canned corn. Kane sat carefully on the box of cans, listening to the old man run down all the information about his bar. He made it clear how people from the music industry came down there all the time in search for new talent.

"Come check it out and bring some cassette tapes with your tracks on it." Next Friday, okay," he instructed. LB smiled and walked away, pointing in Kane's direction. Kane tried to remain cool, but a smile still broke out from the side of his mouth. He replied "Alright," as the last of LB's arm disappeared away from the aisle.

"I'm good just writing lyrics," Kane said later that night when sharing the news with Shyla over the phone. She was not interested and he knew it. She had liked it more when he was selling drugs, being a bad boy.

"Kane, I'm going to South Carolina. My aunt lives there. They want me to go to this community college down there. So—"

"That's cool. For how long?" Kane asked, barely attentive, silently reading off his notepad. Their relationship had gone south months ago. Kane tried in the beginning after Keys' death, but Shyla was too stuck on the old Kane.

In anger Shyla, slammed the phone down. She knew he wasn't really listening.

———

Hours later.

Kane heard the sound of a car driving over the wet pavement in front of Jade's apartment building. It was two in the morning—he was still up rhyming. He wanted to change some of the lyrics around to disguise Justice's name. He also removed some of the curses, afraid of what the crowd might think.

Jade walked up to the living room. "Kane," Jade paused, "get some sleep!" He looked up, too tired to be startled, and then nodded "yes" in silence. She fixed her scarf across her head and headed back to bed. Tomorrow night was the big night. Frost had given Kane the morning shift tomorrow. Everything was set.

Hours passed.

Kane tossed and turned all night, knocking his feet against the day-bed in the living room. It was now 4:00am. His eyes continuously flickered; his nightmare was in full swing.

"Kane, Kane!" Jade shouted, jumping across the bed with her face drained from a lack of sleep. Trevor stood near the entranceway, frowning. Kane recoiled; hitting his head against the corner post. He awoke, finding himself soaked in sweat.

"Yo, he needs to stop making so much noise," Trevor complained loud enough so Kane could hear, then headed back into the bedroom.

"Jade," Kane said, sitting up calmly, "I dreamt all my teeth were falling out. Strange, huh? Then I was buried alive, trying to dig myself out. Then… then, he grabbed my hand"

"Who did?" Jade asked, tired but concerned.

"Keys, but he was wearing black stuff all over his face. And the woman, she was pulling me too, but I didn't want to go with them. They said I wasn't ready then they let my hand go. It was a dream?" Kane's eyes widened as he sat across the bed. To him it felt like something more.

"Kane, that's because you're nervous about tomorrow…well, today. It's almost morning. Try not to worry. You'll be fine." Jade stood up and headed back to the room for some much-needed sleep. She had spent most of her night dealing with Trevor's drunkenness. Ever since he had crashed his Jeep, he had been drinking more. Moreover, since the police were constantly patrolling the area, his heroin business had slowed to a crawl. He was such a nice guy when they had first met. She'd been looking for the old Trevor for three years now.

Kane checked the clock on the VCR and tried to fall back to sleep.

—

Finally, it was Kane's big night.

"Listen man, you're up after him," LB said sharply, bringing more butterflies to Kane's stomach. He looked over at the guy that was next—an R&B singer for certain. His brown and white MC Hammer pants with a white glittering vest gave it away. It actually looked pretty cool. MC hammer had the number one record out; it was perfect for the crowd. Kane was dressed in the jean suit he bought while hustling for Justice. It was a safe choice.

"Okay, you ready?" LB asked, talking to the R&B singer next to Kane. All the performers were carefully parked in a corner backstage, laughing and talking. None of them seemed nervous. It was obvious that it wasn't their first time. The bar was packed; occupied by anxious onlookers that came from all over the city—a nice place to party.

He heard the opening beat of "Can You Stand the Rain," as the singer prepared for his opening. He confidently collected the microphone from the stand as the crowd moved closer to the stage. Kane fell back, remembering the good ole days with Shyla. He loved that song. He reminisced over the first time they met. He still loved her, but they were falling apart fast. *I'll call her after the show; maybe I'll even take a taxi to her house*, Kane thought, as he watched the bouncy singer spin around the microphone.

JC, was the singer's stage name, he twirled around the mic-stand and continued amusing the crowd with his Johnny Gill-esque performance. When he finished, the bar vibrated from the applause. Whistles and screams echoed from the back wall. They loved him.

"Good luck," JC said to Kane. He returned backstage, his face dripping with sweat. Kane welcomed the support. In fact, all the contestants seemed overly nice and supportive, something Kane needed, considering the palm of his hands were soaked in sweat.

"Now, are you ready for some hard core music straight from the streets of BK?" LB screamed over the crowd after the acronym left his mouth. There seemed to be a strong Brooklyn presence. Kane hoped none of them were from his old neighborhood. The last thing he needed was to be noticed by someone who knew Justice.

"Well, I've got a treat for you tonight," LB said, raising his voice as the Naughty by Nature instrumental beat lifted the crowd from their seats. The walls throbbed with each beat. "Welcome Ka-Ron!" He backed off the stage as Kane grabbed the microphone with conviction.

It was the Hip Hop Hooray beat. Kane strolled across the stage, rhyming with such force, the energy caused the stage to wobble. The roar of the crowd was deafening and the rest of the contestants backstage raced in for a look. Everyone was engrossed as Kane continued to deliver his electrifying performance. His voice was something new—unique, different from anything out at the moment.

He kept up the same energy through both of his performances, and when it was over, he maintained his bad boy image by leaving the stage without a thank you to the crowd. It was just a show business stunt. In reality, his mouth kept quivering, trying to keep from smiling.

LB sported an uncontrollable grin, as he tried to introduce the next contestant. He left the stage to find Kane.

"Yo, youngster, I don't know what to say. I mean…shit, man!" Kane leaned against the wall, listening to LB talk about his future at the bar and in the music industry. LB was one of the few good people left who was still partially working in the industry. He was smart and everyone loved him because he was honest. Many of the stars whose careers began in his bar came back to perform a song or two there occasionally as a favor. He had pictures of artists from James Brown to New Edition hanging on his navy-blue walls.

LB told Kane that he had a new home there. Although he could not pay him much, he vowed to introduce Kane to the right people when it was time. Kane wondered: *How did he come up with a cool name like Ka-Ron? I like it!*

He called Shyla, flushed with excitement but she wasn't home. He tried beeping her, but still nothing. It was a clear sign that their relationship had hit a tipping point.

Weeks passed.

Then months.

Kane's fame had grown. He even had a separate show from the other contestants. It was only a matter of time before the music industry noticed him. LB was coaching him every step of the way.

Although Kane and Shyla did not officially break up, it was months since they last saw each other. Frost became Kane's new best friend. Frost lived in the basement of his aunt's house. It made for the perfect bachelor pad and, because it was only two blocks away from Jade's apartment, it was the perfect place for him to go to escape Trevor's drunken outbursts.

"Hey, listen Kay," LB said, pulling him off to the side one night. Kane always listened with a keen ear whenever LB spoke. The bar was nearly empty, after another great performance.

LB led Kane to a booth seat normally reserved for VIPs during business hours. "Listen, I think you're ready. I have some people I want you to meet on Monday!"

"Who, Fred Johnson and them?" Kane asked with a puzzled look, still trying to fix himself straight in the booth. Numerous people who had claimed to work for a record label had approached him. Kane took LB's advice and always ignored them. Kane was an ex-hustler himself and was used to people trying to hustle him.

"No, son," LB said, smirking as he explained the situation to Kane. A new, up and coming record label that only had a handful of fresh artists was interested. A smaller label, which was perfect for a startup artist like Kane. It was clear LB didn't want Kane to sign a big contract just yet.

"Let us see how the first single goes, then we'll go for the big fish," LB explained. He was smart and he liked Kane—and for good reason.

Kane, during his months working the stage, had never asked for anything. LB's bar had gotten so crowded on Fridays they had to remove most of the seats. It was no secret that the crowd came primarily to see Kane perform.

They talked over a few drinks then he headed for home. Monday was the big day. Kane smiled from ear to ear. His dream—their dream, his and Keys' was coming true.

⌐

Later on at his sister's apartment.

"Bitch, I told you to stop fucking asking me about—" Kane heard Trevor's drunken voice from the other side of the door. He sighed.

*Not tonight.*

He opened the front door.

He considered going to Frost's, but then he glanced over and saw the fresh bruise below his sister's right eye. She was fixed on the floor near the front door, crying uncontrollably. Kane quickly came to her aid, seething.   He knew Trevor was behind it.

Gently, he lifted his sister's face. The bruise was awful. His mouth tightened with rage.

"Oh, no, no, Kane!" Jade pleaded with him as he sprang up and headed for the living room.

Trevor heard the commotion and headed back towards Jade. He suspected it was Kane and was all set to fight.

"Jade, close the fucking door!" Trevor screamed out.

Kane fell to his knees, looking beneath the day bed for his gun.

*"Got it!"* He muttered.

He headed straight for Trevor's babbling voice. "I've been wanting to do this for years," Kane said as his fist clutched the black 9mm pistol.

They met.

He smacked the side of Trevor's head with the gun handle.

Then again on top of his forehead.

Trevor's body collapsed against the hallway wall, yet Kane continued his attack. He dealt more blows to Trevor's nose and then to the back of his ear. He stood alarmingly calm as he continued to size up each blow.

He looked for more open shots, through Trevor's feeble defense.

"Got one," Kane said quietly, as he hit him across his right temple. It knocked him out cold. Trevor's body slid lifelessly to the floor as blood poured from his face.

"Kane! What did you do? What did you do?" Jade shouted, falling next to Trevor's body, which was still trembling in shock from the beating. Kane stood there, breathing heavy, thinking of all the times Jade had called the house in tears. He thought of Justice and Majestic, how they had killed Keys in cold blood. He had snapped. He stood over Trevor, out of breath.

"Kane, just leave! Just leave!" Jade said, crying over Trevor's body. Kane slowly walked into the living room and packed up his things. He knew the cops and ambulance would be there shortly to ask questions. He left, heading to Frost's house.

Moments later.

"You alright man?" Frost asked, opening the front door to his basement apartment.

"Yeah, I'm good. I need to stay here for a few days though," Kane said softly, resting his bag by the TV stand.

"Yeah, man, I told you that you can stay here anytime," Frost said as he headed to the refrigerator for some Budweisers.

—

Meanwhile, back at Jade's apartment.

The ambulance finally found their way. "Where's the patient?" The rude medic asked, looking more frustrated than worried.

"He's over there," Jade said as she led the way, still crying. Trevor was unconscious but still breathing.

"Okay, Miss," the cop asked her, "what happened here?" He was unfazed by Jade's oversized bruise or the tears that poured down her face and before she could answer him, they all turned their attention to the medic's voice in the hallway. "Okay, Okay, that's it," he said. They had given Trevor some smelling salts. He was beginning to regain consciousness. He was still dazed as the medic gently began removing some of the blood from his face. He was still too confused to remember everything, but managed to mutter, "I'm good. I'm good."

A half-hearted smile crossed her face when she heard his voice. She began wiping tears away and turned back towards the cops. "It was a fight," she said, thinking of Kane. She didn't want him arrested. It would have been a serious assault charge. "He was hitting on me, so I picked up the glass ash tray and hit him." Jade told the new story convincingly and the cops tried to keep from smiling. Domestic abuse charges were so common in this neighborhood, their next question to her was about her pressing charges. She nodded her head "yes." The cop sized her up quickly and continued taking notes.

As Trevor passed through the front door with the medics, their eyes met. It said a million words. His eyes said, "This is not over. I'm going to get you, you bitch," and hers simply said, "We're done."

Jade filled out a report with the police, and requested an Order of Protection be put on him. She got one, easily. She returned home from the police precinct and packed up all of his stuff, called his cousin the same night and told him to come get his things. They were through and she did not want to give him any reason to come back.

# Chapter Eleven

MONDAY HAD FINALLY ARRIVED; Kane's big day with the record company. "Come in. Kane is it?" A white gentleman asked, holding the glass door open for him. The man was well-dressed in an all-black suit, black shirt and black tie. He had a nice trendy look to him and was very articulate. Kane walked in eyeing the G&G Records sign displayed neatly across the door. Just under that was "Robert Williamson, CEO."

Already impressed by the company's location, in the heart of Manhattan, he sat down anxious, trying to keep cool.

"Larry!" Mr. Williamson said, already familiar with LB as they shook hands. LB sent him Kane's music weeks ago.

They wasted no time getting down to business.

They talked for hours and went over every inch of the contract.

They discussed everything from studio time to shows and royalties. When the meeting ended, Mr. Williamson's hair was flattened with sweat. The deal was done and both sides were relatively happy.

Kane agreed to cut two singles for the label. The total deal was worth $250,000. When Kane heard the number, he needed every ounce of self-control not to jump across the table and hug Mr. Williamson. They both settled for an overly-active handshake. Kane grinned from ear to ear. He still could not believe it. He collected LB's jacket from the floor and tried to keep from jumping up and down.

"Kane, again, are you good with this?" LB asked him with a serious look as he passed Kane the contract for signatures. Kane grinned and then asked, "I mean, what do you think? Is it good?"

"Yes, I think it's good. It's a good start rather," LB said seriously. He knew everything about the industry. He knew all about bad contracts, getting a few thousand for shows when the profits were in the hundred thousands. He had managed many people and made his share of mistakes—but not today. It was a good deal.

Weeks passed.

Kane stayed at Frost's house. He kept most of his money in the bank but managed some new clothes, a black Pathfinder, and some modest jewelry—a few gold rings and one heavy, gold-link chain. Frost became his right hand man. They both quit Fresco's Supermarket when his first check arrived. Wanting to learn as much as possible about making music, he spent most of his time in the studio with producers and music makers.

He was thrilled, about everything; except needing permission to perform at LB's bar. It was part of the contract that the record label decide the venues where he performs. Kane still stopped by LB's every chance he could—inconspicuously arriving in the back—to get some advice from the wise man.

He sent money to Jade, asking her to give some to their mother. He knew his mother would never believe he'd made the money honestly. Jade was doing just fine without Trevor. Kane had beaten Trevor so badly it kept him in the hospital for weeks. He talked every day about what he would do when he got out, but when he was finally released, nothing came of it. Jade went back to school for nursing. Rumor had it she was dating one of the male nurses at the training center. Finally, a nice guy.

"So, are they cool with you performing at LB's spot tomorrow?" Frost asked, worried as he laced up the new Timberland boots Kane just bought for him.

"Yeah, man, what did I tell you? I just can't do any songs under my contr—," Kane paused and looked at Frost in disbelief. Their eyes locked on each other in shock. The opening to Kane's first single finally hit the radio.

"Turn it up! Turn it up! Oh, shit!" Kane said, falling over the Sega game console. They both jumped up and down, shouting out the lyrics at the top of their lungs. Kane was still shaking from excitement hours after the song finished. It was a definite hit.

The radio jockey played it repeatedly throughout the night. But, Kane was unaware that his record had been playing a few days before on different stations.

—

The following night at LB's club.

Kane, eyeing Frost from backstage, watched his friend try to pick up another batch of girls at the bar. Frost's newfound confidence drove him to flirt with nearly every woman he passed. He asked Frost to get him a rum and coke, a drink he'd knock back before each performance to loosen him up

"Fucking guy," Kane said, annoyed. He pushed the curtain back slightly and headed over to the bar.

There were two artists performing ahead of him. He had enough time. "Yo, man," Kane said, catching up with Frost, "I told you—"

A girl's voice interrupted him.

"Kane?"

"Shyla?" Kane asked, puzzled.

He wasn't sure it was her. She looked different. She wore a noticeably short mini dress and had too much makeup on. A bit tasteless from the way he remembered her. She stood next to a much older guy—in his forties perhaps. His heart raced. He still had feelings for her, and struggled to hide the awkwardness of the situation. He kept his eyes sideways, closer to Frost. Looking straight into her eyes was too painful.

"Can I get you a drink?" Kane asked, trying to be polite.

"Nah, I got that young blood," the older man said. Frost openly stared at the man with disgust. He was clearly a pimp or an old-time thug from the streets. Kane knew the type from his hustling days.

*Shyla always loved the streets. I guess it was just a matter of time before it became her life.*

"Well, I'm just here to hear that record, you know Act Like You Know," Shyla said, referring to Kane's hit single. She had no idea.

"Yeah," Kane said, grabbing the drink from Frost, "I know that song." He headed backstage in disbelief. He still wore the jeans she gave him for his birthday.

Moments later.

"Fellas! Ladies! Welcome to the stage, the man who needs no intro. With all of his success, he hasn't forgotten us. Ka-Ron!" LB stated, happily. He bounced off the stage as the opening beat came in from Kane's hit single. He wasn't supposed to do that song, but LB was a good friend. Kane kept his loyalty to the man. Besides, his record sales were sky rocketing. *What could they possibly do to the rising star?*

As Kane walked onstage, the crowd exploded, pushing towards the stage area as he started in with his opening delivery. They screamed so loud, he was barely heard over the microphone.

Shyla's mouth widened with shocked. A deep hurt penetrated her chest as she fell against the bar, looking for a stool to sit on. She sat down fighting back tears. Unable to bear the sight of him, she turned towards the bar and began playing with her apple martini. She thought he'd become a loser. She regretted every time she changed the subject when he talked about his music. She regretted everything.

Kane performed both his hit songs without a glance in her direction. They both knew their relationship was now officially over.

# Chapter Twelve

KANE EXITED THE STUDIO BOOTH as Curtis Jones, his music director, waved him over. Two years had passed, and Kane was a full-blown star. He and Frost had moved to Hollywood a year ago. Frost was still charming women and had opened a bar in Manhattan with the money Kane gave him. He saved much of his profits. He wanted to keep it to repay Kane some day. Their friendship was based on loyalty, which started to resemble the relationship he had with Keys.

Kane had moved his mother and Jade into a house in Queens. He sent money to Craig every few months, as well. His family was well-taken care of and, as for Kane, he had a three-million dollar house equipped with all that money could buy: three live-in maids, and an indoor swimming pool modeled from the pool in the 'New Jack City' movie. His triple platinum albums made him a frontrunner for several movie roles. He was becoming a mega star, with a line of artists dying to record a duet with him. However, LB made all the decisions. Kane forced him out of his bar and back into the music business full-time. LB's brother was running his club for him back in New York.

Kane, a boy from one of the most dangerous projects in Brooklyn, was estimated to make more money than half the people in Hollywood in the next five years. He never kept a steady girl after Shyla. Besides, LB didn't leave him much time for anything but work. When he heard that Justice had been convicted, serving a life sentence, he finally felt some closure with his past. However, Keys was never forgotten. After every performance, he paid tribute to him. Management had asked him to stop now that he was in mainstream Hollywood, but he refused.

"Yo," Kane said, closing the studio door behind him, smiling across at Roxy Rose. Roxy Rose was a two-time Grammy winner, a mega star in the States and abroad. She was a pop singer, but rapped as well. They released their duet two weeks ago. It sold out in London, most of the U.S., and parts of Brazil. Roxy Rose was Brazilian, but moved to the States when she was eleven. She was beautiful. If she was not dating the actor, Robert Dane, Kane would have made his move months ago.

"Well, everyone knows why we're here," stated Curtis. The little room was packed with producers, video directors, and managers. Their managers thought it would be a good idea to meet one last time before they flew out to Rio de Janeiro to shoot the video for the duet. Roxy and Kane thought it was silly. They'd planned this trip a month ago and had been speaking on the phone nearly every day. It surely did not require Kane to fly to New York, but their managers thought of the bright idea.

Roxy and Kane impatiently listened to all the concerns in the room. They repeated what they had discussed about this trip weeks ago. They would all assemble in Miami next Friday and take a private jet to Rio. From there they would all be driven to a rented house on the coast in Sao Conrado, Brazil. The actual video would be shot on the famous

Copacabana Beach. The managers ran down the security plans and the schedule for a fifth time.

Roxy and Kane cast aside their manager's foolish carefulness and began talking. Although she had skin so fair, it was practically white and his skin was dark, they would have made a handsome couple. The video was sure to be a hit.

"When are you flying back?" Roxy asked Kane, smiling across at her manager's childish scowl.

"Ah, tomorrow. They have me working twenty-four hours a day. We're trying to clean up this track before next week." Kane had to discipline himself not to look at her breasts. Roxy's figure was staggering and she accentuated it more by wearing tiny tops and skin-tight jeans.

"Oh! Wanna go party tonight?" Roxy asked, excited. "I can teach you more Portuguese," she coaxed him; gently tugging Kane's hand. She'd been teaching him some words in Portuguese over the phone, but he always pronounced them incorrectly the very next time they spoke.

"Yeah, alright. Where?" Kane asked, trying to keep from smiling too hard. He was dying to have a moment alone with her.

They meet later that night at a small bar right below the penthouse at the Sheraton Hotel, along Seventh Avenue.

"What's wrong?" An attractive redhead asked, placing her hand on Kane's left leg. The bar had been closed to the public and was occupied by a few stars and some loyal, very attractive groupies. However, Kane had been to these parties before. He knew there would be lots of snorting coke, dancing, and sex—none of which he ever participated in. LB and the crack-cocaine streets had taught him better.

"Nothing, just chilling," Kane said, trying not to be rude. Most of the people were there for Roxy, but they knew who he was. It was not his type of crowd, and without Frost, he felt compelled to leave early. Glancing over at the bar, he smirked when he saw a woman's bare breast. He'd seen worse. These parties were never complete until someone was having sex in front of everyone. He turned back to the Manhattan skyline, thinking about his childhood in New York.

It wasn't long ago that he was playing basketball with Dimitri and Tileyah. Tileyah. *Where is she now?* He hadn't seen her in over three years. Tileyah, his first. Looking back, he realized that it may have been one of the best nights of his life.

"Where do you think you're going?" Roxy asked, drunk, collecting Kane by the waist. Her boyfriend never minded her flirtatious behavior; they were both wild and crazy. With a passionate eye, she invited him closer as they stood facing each other. Kane was instantly aroused, and calmly wrapped his arms around her waist, smiling. The embarrassing bulge from his pants rubbed against her zipper.

"I'll be right back. I need to see a friend," Kane said, softly stroking her back with his left hand. He touched the lower part of her waist and pressed her in tighter. Clearly turned on, she slowly moved away from his hold, embarrassed. Normally, that wouldn't bother her, but Kane got the sense that she actually liked him.

"Okay, come back though. I want to talk with you!" Roxy said, looking around, feeling self-conscious.

Kane walked out of the party.

He headed for the projects in Brooklyn in search of Tileyah. *Does she look any good now,* he wondered as he pressed the button in the elevator.

At one point Tileyah loved him. Looking back, he knew it to be true. He did not know when he would be in New York again; it was the best time to visit her. Most of the people he now hung out with were from LA and Miami. So much time had passed that he had no clue what to expect. The last he heard of her was through Craig. He'd heard that she started attending a community college in Queens.

*Man, the block looks different.* Kane watched in amazement as his black, tinted Cadillac slowly inched in front of his old building. The block was much different. Most of the benches were gone, and the skelly court, which once covered the cement, was deeply faded. The building was in worse condition with the front door nearly falling off its hinges. Strange new people crowded the front entrance. They looked like thugs up to no good.

"Dooley," Kane said, smirking as he recognized a familiar face dribbling a basketball near the side of the tree. A light mist of sweat trickled from the white driver's forehead as Kane rolled down the back window. Double parked in front of this building would frighten most people.

"Yo, Dooley!" Kane yelled. There were newcomers on the block. If they knew it was the infamous "Ka-Ron," there was no telling what would happen. Dooley had lived on the first floor—a good kid. Kane never paid too much attention to him growing up; he was much younger at the time.

"Kay! Ka-Ron!" Dooley shouted with excitement as he dropped the basketball.

"Nah! Nah!" Kane said, trying to keep his presence a secret. He invited him into the car. *Wow, it's funny what three years could do.* Kane looked up, shocked about Dooley's new height. He was a little kid when Kane last saw him. He was much older now. The oversized kid reminded him of the days of skelly and basketball. So much had changed. There were only a few kids outside, and they stood around aimlessly.

"Yo, I can't believe it's you man. Shit!" Dooley said, still in shock. Kane kept an oversized smile while he listened to Dooley run down what he had missed over the past few years.

"And Tileyah? What's up with her?" Kane questioned with a more serious look.

"Oh, she use to come by here about a year ago, but I haven't seen her in a while. Her mother still lives here though. I can run upstairs and ask her," Dooley added, still energized by Kane's presence, twitching in his seat.

"That would be cool. Yeah, can you?" Kane answered, wearing that movie star smile; teeth white, hair freshly cut, and an oversized gold link chain with a cross.

Minutes later, Dooley returned with a piece of paper detailing the direction and address of Tileyah's place.

Queens!

Kane eyed the paper and grimaced. He didn't want to go on a scavenger hunt, looking for this girl.

*I came this far, I might as well head over there. Besides, my mother lives in Queens. I'll have the driver call her on the car phone if I can't find Tileyah.* Kane went over the details in his head. He gave Dooley fifty dollars for his help. He'd always been generous, even in his hustling days. He had loaned Keys money all the time. Now, Frost practically got anything he wanted.

Hours later, wheels rolled over gravel, inches from the sidewalk.

After fighting through traffic on the Grand Central Parkway, they finally arrived at Tileyah's.

The driver waited in silence, as Kane directed him to stay put. He opened the back door himself. The driver had been frustrated by Kane's sudden quest to find Tileyah, but he felt much more comfortable at this location.

*Number 234, this is it.* Kane confirmed the address with the paper again. The block was empty; there was not a soul in sight. Typical suburbs. A smile of relief crossed Kane's face as his fingers connected with the doorbell.

Kane waited quietly, placing one foot back off the front step. Suddenly the hallway light appeared beneath the door. Kane's heartbeat lifted as the doorknob began to turn.

"Tileyah," Kane said quietly. She trembled in disbelief. Unable to speak, she lingered at the front door, eyes open wide. As he eyed her belly, a sharp pain traveled through his chest.

She was pregnant. Trying to break the awkward moment, he said, "Well, aren't you going to invite me in?"

"Who's at the—?" Dimitri asked, unable to finish his question as he arrived at the front door. He paused and a broken smile was frozen on his face.

"Dimitri?" Kane shouted in excitement, completely closing his eyes to them being a couple and having a baby on the way. Dimitri was too cool to get angry with. In the end, he was just trying to catch up on old times.

"Come in. Come in," Dimitri instructed, passionately. Tileyah was still in shock, holding the top of her head with both hands as Kane made his way in.

Kane was praying for an untroubled night and it was just that. They talked for hours, evoking everything that was good and bad about their childhood. Dimitri talked the most, and his eyes wore the truth. He loved Kane; they were the best of friends above everything else. Tileyah was clearly uncomfortable. It was clear that she still loved him.

Dimitri understood her feelings and smartly looked passed her mood. Now that Kane, the mega-star, was in his house, jealousy would be a natural response from Dimitri, but he admired Kane too much. Besides, he knew Kane wouldn't disrespect their situation and he was right. Kane skillfully stayed away from the subject of his short but romantic history with Tileyah. Dimitri headed for the refrigerator, asking Kane if he wanted another beer. Seconds later, he handed Kane an ice-cold Heineken and headed for the bathroom.

Possibly the only chance they would have to speak privately. "Listen," Kane said softly, "I want to tell you that I'm sorry. For everything. I was young." His eyes turned down towards the table as he played with a beer cap. He was never good at expressing himself this way, even after three years.

Tileyah stood up abruptly in anger. "You know, Kane, this was supposed to be our life," Tileyah said; her voice cracked in anguish. She strode away from the kitchen. She couldn't bear the sight of him anymore.

"You were my first and I loved you," Tileyah said, turning around as her eyes began to swell with tears.

Kane leaned back in his chair and lifted his bottle of Heineken, trying to hide the swell of emotions he felt.

The toilet flushed. Dimitri returned, unfazed by Tileyah's disappearance. He knew she was upset. He ignored it completely.

He headed for the refrigerator for another beer, still excited by Kane's presence. "I'll have one more, then I gotta run, Dee." Tileyah's announcement had stunned him. They were true lovers. Were they supposed to be with each other? Kane's thoughts kept spiraling at the idea.

They talked for awhile, mainly about Kane's career and Hollywood. *It was an interesting night,* Kane thought to himself, waving to Dimitri from the back of the car. His eyes fixed on the second floor window. He couldn't help but notice Tileyah's silhouette standing off to the side. "Bye-Tileyah," he whispered softly.

# Chapter Thirteen

FEET SPLASHED THROUGH PUDDLES. The rain continued to fall as the ground crew fell into position. It had been raining in Miami for days, and the newly deployed private jet had finally been cleared to take off after two long hours. They all quickly made their way onto the plane. Roxy's hands were empty. Her assistant lugged her carry-on. She was a true diva when she wanted to be.

Kane had unwisely chosen to wear his light blue, suede-covered timberlands, which were now soaked from the rain. Overall, he seemed a bit overdressed for the long flight to Rio de Janeiro. Listening to Frost never did him any good.

Moments later.

"Ms. Rose, we're sorry for the delay. We just got clearance and should be off the ground in twenty minutes." The captain had personally apologized to Roxy as she entered the plane. The captain practically ignored Kane's presence. He didn't mind. It was Roxy's thing—he just had a small part at the end of the video. Most of the expenses were under her company anyway. The jet was fairly new and was equipped with all the luxuries for the typical Hollywood star, but it wasn't impervious to the weather. The plane stood on the runway for another thirty minutes.

"Damn! How long is it going to be? Shit!" Frost complained aloud, looking out the window at the falling rain. Kane tried to get comfortable by resting his feet on top of the cream-colored coffee table, but it didn't work. He continued fidgeting around in his seat.

Finally, there was word from the captain.

"Again, my apologies for the delay. Prepare for takeoff," the captain said energetically. The five passengers began to fix themselves for the flight, snapping in their seatbelts and turning their seats forward.

It would be Kane and Frost's first time out of the States. He gazed out of the window, straining to see through the dense fog. He made out a few palm trees blowing in the wind. "Wow, finally leaving the States," he whispered to himself. He clutched his chair as the plane started down the slippery runway. He flew enough to anticipate a rocky take off in this weather. He shut his eyes quickly and pulled down the window shade as the plane picked up more speed.

The plane was now airborne, on its way to a cruising altitude of 27,000 feet or so. Sounds of the kitchen service trays slammed against the wall, nothing unusual considering the winds.

The turbulence continued.

It got heavier.

Suddenly, the plane dipped sharply.

Kane clutched his armrest in pure terror. He hated flying. He never became accustomed to the rocks and trembles of an airplane during flight.

The plane continued to dip, as if it was out of control. The unsuspecting jerks forced his left hand to seize the top portion of the arm rest. The last dip even caught the attention of Roxy's adventurous boyfriend, Robert Dane, who never passed up a chance to go sky diving. He sat up, alarmed.

The plane jerked again.

They could all feel the freshly made jet gliding to the left, struggling through the cloud cover.

"Fuck, Fuck!" Frost muttered in fear, tucked down in his seat.

"Please have your seat belts fastened," the captain warned.

The turbulence continued. It seemed endless, though the plane had not been off the ground for more than four minutes.

Kane was now in full panic from the turmoil. He crumpled down into his seat and held both armrests in utter shock.

The seat belt alarm continued to go off. The captain had left it on by accident. It took the sound of a May Day call, as if the plane was going down—adding to the mayhem.

*Please, won't someone turn that irritating beeping noise off?* Roxy pleaded silently.

They endured the agonizing beeping sound and food carts banging against the wall for thirty minutes. It felt like an eternity, but it was now over. The plane finally reached a safe distance above the storm system, which delivered some much needed tranquility. At least for the moment.

Meanwhile, in the cockpit.

"Ted, run a diagnostic on our landing gear and check the navigation system too." The captain ordered his co-pilot. He feared something might have become unfixed during that hellish event. *I guess the Air Traffic Controllers didn't realize the strength of the storm,* the captain thought to himself.

"Captain, the navigation…," Ted paused, as he continued looking at the reading. "Oh, okay. We're good," he said, relieved that the results of the test had read correctly on the console after a bizarre glitch.

"What the fuck!" Frost yelled, no longer trying to conceal his anxiousness. "We should land, right now. Fuck that!" Frost came loose as he unfastened his belt, ready to storm the cockpit area.

"Chill," Kane said in a shaky tone. He understood his concern completely, but the plane was seemingly safe for now.

*What happened?*

*Should they still be flying or trying to land?*

As the captain overheard the commotion, he asked his co-pilot, to take over as he stepped out to address the restless passengers.

"I'm deeply sorry. The turbulence was rather heavy and unexpected. We are above the storm system now and shouldn't feel much of anything," he stated, then tried to lighten the mood. "Please, have a drink or two drinks. Enjoy the rest of the flight," he finished, smiling. He pulled the flight attendant closer to him. "Take good care of them," the captain ordered then ducked back into the cockpit. Everyone was relieved the moment was over; they sat poking fun at each other.

Two hours had passed.

Nearly everyone was sound asleep. Kane was the only one with fresh eyes. He stared out the window watching the sun slip below the thick line of clouds.

Ten minutes later the sky was a dark blue. They would be in Rio in a few hours.

Meanwhile, in the cockpit.

"Captain, I think we may have an issue here," the co-pilot said, staring at the navigational console as the screen began flickering. They eyed each other in shock as the navigational console suddenly went black.

They were not sure about their position and needed confirmation.

"Command Station 2, Command Station 2, this is 9-0-9-8 bird. Repeat, this is 9-0-9-8 bird. Can you confirm our current position?" The captain talked clearly into his headpiece, as the co-pilot fought to keep his composure.

Suddenly, the co-pilot bounced out of his seat. He watched in disbelief, as the communication console lost power. First, the navigation system then the communication system. The plane seemed to be suffering from an electrical shortage. There was no telling what would go next.

"Command Station 2, Command Station 2, this is 9-0-9-8 bird; repeat, this is 9-0-9-8 bird. Please advise Command Station 2," the captain lifted his voice and repeated again.

The captain kept cool, but he knew what could happen next—the engines could shut off.

Before notifying the passengers, they had to come up with a plan. If their navigation system had the correct reading, before it went blank, they could fly east and try an emergency landing on the edge of northern Brazil. They were in extreme danger by flying with no direction and no communications, at their current altitude. They made a decision to fly at a low altitude to avoid a collision with another plane.

The captain turned on the seat belt alarm.

"Please fasten your seat belts," the captain instructed quickly. There was no time to explain everything now.

Suddenly, the plane began a wild descent.

Everyone awoke.

Frost grimaced as he snapped in his seat belt.

The plane felt like it was on a free fall, not a descent.

The flight attendant looked anxiously toward the cockpit. Roxy Rose's boyfriend dashed to the cockpit, demanding an answer from the captain. He had no plans of staying strapped to his seat without an explanation.

A stiff jolt swung his body into the lavatory.

Everyone began screaming.

Climbing out of the restroom, Robert pounded on the door, demanding a word with the captain.

"Please," the flight attendant said, desperately. "Please sit down, sir!" However, he stood by the cockpit door and continued to knock.

The plane jerked again.

Then again.

Roxy recoiled in her seat, too petrified to move. She clutched her assistant, Julie, who was screaming for dear life.

Meanwhile, in the cockpit.

"Listen, once we get beneath the clouds, I'll have a long talk with the passengers," the captain assured the co-pilot, whose eyes were glued to Robert's hammering against the cockpit door. The captain, strained, tried to keep control of the aircraft, as the main steering seemed to be slipping from his grasp. The air was thick, and they were coming down too fast.

Minutes later.

They cleared the clouds, finally.

The black of the Atlantic Ocean painted all sides of the window. Kane peeked out. But, there was nothing to see, just the ocean in total darkness, roaring from the storm. The plane finally settled into calm, but for how long?

"Ted," the captain said, lightly handing over the controls to the restless co-pilot. He braced himself to deal with five very anxious passengers.

The cockpit door opened.

The captain's shirt was drenched in sweat.

Robert stood in front of him before he could manage a second step out of the cockpit. The captain gave him an icy glare, clearly frustrated by Robert's carelessness. "Please sit down, sir!" He could have been seriously injured not being fastened in his seat.

With no communication from Air Traffic Control, they had no idea of the storm's severity. It was, in fact, a "category four" storm. It was a miracle that the plane was not strewn in pieces over the Atlantic. "Listen, please calm down," the captain shouted over the cursing, primarily coming from Frost and Robert.

"I'm not going to lie to you all. The plane is with a problem. We have lost all communication and all navigational systems, including backup systems. We believe the initial turbulence during takeoff, may have been the root cause. Based on our speed and the last reliable reading, we believe we are just east of Trinidad & Tobago." The captain explained his plan carefully while the shocked passengers listened intently.

Kane was in complete shock. He could not believe the words coming from the captain's mouth. *This cannot be happening,* Kane thought to himself.

"We have more than enough fuel. It's just a matter of finding a place to land. We are below the system now. We are trying to contact the Brazilian and Caribbean Air traffic control or their governments. I will keep you posted every half hour on our status." The captain was very convincing, although he had to deal with a ton of questions. He answered all of them with honesty.

The plane was steady and unusually quiet at its current altitude; they were only 14,000 feet above the ocean. It was a dangerous position, but they had no choice. They had to fly that low to avoid a mid-air collision with another plane.

"Fuck, we going to die! They don't know where the fuck we are," Frost said frantically. He tried to hold back the tears from his eyes, but could not any longer. He turned his head to face the window.

As promised, the captain updated them nearly ten times over the past few hours, but there had been no true improvement in their situation. To make matters worst, the view from their windows remained black from the night which added another layer of uncertainty and terror to the situation.

Kane stayed quiet the entire time, thinking of his father, then Keys. He tried to grab some courage from it. Roxy, in a daze, kept her eyes close shut. There were no more tears left; everyone was numb. It was truly hell.

Five hours passed.

Then nearly another five.

Over ten hours had passed since the captain said they were looking for a safe place to land.

Nothing.

They'd been on the plane for over thirteen hours; everyone started thinking the same thing. Do we have enough fuel?

Meanwhile, in the cockpit.

The captain stared at the auxiliary fuel tank gage in total exhaustion. Ted was asleep. The overworked captain planned to wake him soon. Suddenly, a hint of sun edged its way up over the horizon. The captain found a small smile beneath his fatigue. They had a better chance of finding somewhere to land in daylight. He tapped his co-pilot on the shoulder to give him the good news, and then glanced at the fuel gage reading again.

It read, three thousand pounds of reserve fuel left.

How could that be?

Just seconds ago, it had read 9,120 pounds. The captain was spent. The plane was unreliable. If the gage was correct, they had just twenty minutes to land or the weary plane would stall out and land for them. He quickly silenced the emergency alarm before it could ring. Once the fuel fell below a thousand pounds, the alarm would have sounded. The captain did not want another plane-wide panic attack.

Just then, Ted shouted, "There!" He was pointing out the left window. The captain looked and saw an enormous land mass that stretched for miles, but the coast was still miles away. Would they have enough fuel to make the landing?

The captain charged out of the cockpit to deliver the news. He didn't think there was any point in mentioning the low fuel situation, but he asked the flight-attendant to describe all the emergency procedures in detail to the passengers. Everyone listened attentively and stayed glued to their seats. They knew it was going to be an unpleasant landing, but were partially relieved to be getting closure.

"Dear God, I'm sorry for all the wrong I've done. If you could find it in your heart to spare us, I promise you that I will try harder to do right," Roxy prayed in Portuguese. Her trembling body nearly shook her seat loose.

Fifteen minutes later, the plane was nearly out of fuel and the land mass was still far away. The captain felt the plane stalling.

They were not going to make land.

"Ted," the captain said in a troubled voice, "We have to go down."
They eyed each other dubiously and began the final descent.

He flicked on the fasten seat belt alarm. Everyone grew to truly
hate that sound.

The plane was traveling nearly 350 miles per hour in a race to land,
but the captain had to slow down now. He pulled up. He'd slow down
as much as he could, but they were still going to hit the Atlantic at over
one hundred miles per hour, fast enough to cause serious damage.

The plane inched near the rocky waters.

2,000 feet.

1,000

500

The plane was dead silent.

Seconds later, the unthinkable.

The plane tumbled 360 degrees across the water. The back wing
tore off like a piece of paper. Silent screams echoed throughout the
plane, only the sound of metal and carbon fiber splitting could be heard
across the Atlantic Ocean.

It tumbled again.

The plane split in two halves. Frost and Julie's bodies were torn
from the plane still in their seats. They were tossed into mid air then
down into the Atlantic. They were gone.

The plane tumbled again, violently.

After endless tumbles, the plane finally rested faintly on the surface
of the ocean. This was just a brief pause before it began its final journey
to the bottom of the ocean.

Water began seeping in quickly.

Roxy was still alive.

She was able to move, but had a piece of metal lodged in her left side—a very gruesome wound. Her flesh was completely exposed with a steady stream of blood flowing from her side. Her boyfriend hadn't been so lucky; his body was crumpled in the corner against the emergency window. He had been thrown from his seat upon impact.

"Roxy!" Kane shouted, struggling to release his seat belt. He was the luckiest soul—nearly unscathed. The captain and his co-pilot died instantly, their necks snapping, during the first tumble. The flight attendant was not immediately visible when Kane first scanned the area. He almost regretted locating her. She was in pieces, beneath the seat in front of him. Her body had been violently severed.

Roxy, still conscious, turned her head towards Kane. He snapped himself free and headed in her direction.

"Hold on, Rox," he said, struggling to unbuckle her seatbelt. The water had begun to rise to their necks. He finally released it. He pulled her from her seat as the plane quickly began sinking. The piece of metal lodged in her side knocked against the chair. There was no time to be careful. Roxy was too weak to cry as Kane's grip tightened around her hand.

"Listen we are going under. You have to hold your breath for a minute or so, okay? Trust me. I got you," Kane said, drawing on his newfound courage. The plane submerged as they struggled out of the back together.

Kane emerged from the water surrounded by tons of debris from the crash. Roxy's head surfaced next to him, barely staying afloat as Kane swung to her rescue. She was still bleeding freely. He quickly grabbed a floating seat behind them. He remembered the flight attendant explaining that the cushions made excellent floating devices. He was about to find out.

He took a long breath, grateful that he was still alive then began to swim toward land with Roxy in tow. It was still nearly two miles away. Although the crash had sent the plane on a long trek of terror and destruction, it brought them closer to shore.

"Look there's land. We can make it," Kane said, collecting a burst of energy, tugging the seat along. Roxy was shivering. Kane took notice of the trail of blood she left behind. She was dying and she knew it. There was no saving her, and the sharks would surely be in the area soon. She was a beach girl; she knew she was risking Kane's life by tagging along.

"Kane," Roxy said in a peaceful voice, "Don't try to rescue me. Just get to shore." "Wait, don't let go. Don't..." Kane pleaded, but then watched as she released the seat and slowly began to sink with the rest of the debris. Kane shook his head slowly from side to side, devastated. He tried to hold his emotions together until he reached land. He grabbed the seat and resumed his lonely voyage ashore.

# Chapter Fourteen

KANE FINALLY STRUGGLED ASHORE. The seat worked for a while, but it seemed to slow him down after the first mile. He abandoned it and swam the last quarter mile, sucking up water.

*Land, finally.*

A deep sigh of relief overpowered his emotions. His eyes watered up. He survived. He gazed at the palm trees winding in the distance.

Brazil?

*If only it was.*

The captain had vastly miscalculated their location. They were never going in the right direction. They were traveling east the entire time, leaving Kane off the shores of Northern Angola—right in the middle of a brutal and endless civil war. He was a long way from Brazil—a long way from home.

Pulling himself ashore with his last bit of strength, he noticed a few men heading in his direction. Help, finally. He sighed with relief as his body collapsed in the wet sand.

Although still flabbergasted by Kane's sudden arrival, Amandio and his motley crew gently helped him out of the wet sand. They stared at each other in disbelief. It was too astonishing for words so they all kept quiet for the moment. A live body crawling onto the shore would stun anyone, but his clothes and jewelry were what truly fascinated them. Kane, an unfortunate victim of Frost's counsel, had worn his very best for his grand entry into Rio de Janeiro. His sky blue Timberlands were still remarkably attached to his feet after the swim. A shining gold-link chain with a massive pendant littered with diamond studs covered his neck and his fingers were no better. They were wrapped with two and three-fingered rings filled with diamonds. Even soaked with water, he still looked fresh. They knew he wasn't from Angola; perhaps not even Africa.

In Portuguese, Amandio asked, "What's your name?" Back in his town just north of Luanda, he had seen pictures of rappers in magazines at a newsstand that carried the South African news. He thought they were African Kings or politicians.

Kane, draped in overpriced jewels and fancy digs, fit the bill of a typical rapper. They knew nothing about rap, but Kane's presence along with his expensive jewelry bewildered them.

"It's a king!" Kgosi assumed, quietly looking over at Kweku. Kweku passionately shook his head no, telling him in a whisper that it was not the time for his father's foolish tales.

Kane was still trying to catch his breath.

"I speak English. I am American. My plane crashed. Can you call the police? My friends are still out there." Kane was muttering a mile a minute. He came to one knee. It was all gibberish to them, except the word American. Even Kweku had learned of that place.

"Americano," said one of the soldiers. He snapped his fingers in excitement.

Kane didn't know what to make of them. They were all carrying AK-47s across their backs, except for Kweku and Kgosi. Kweku, Amandio, and one of his followers were dressed in dark-green army fatigues. *Are they police,* Kane questioned silently, still confused.

Kane was sure he was in Brazil. He had heard Roxy speak to her Brazilian friends over the phone on occasion, and it was clear to him that Amandio was speaking Portuguese. However, the black faces confused him. Black Brazilians, Kane pondered. In his ignorance, he questioned himself silently. Kane was not much of a student of Brazil; he trusted what he had picked up from Frost's stories.

"Please," Kane pleaded, turning towards Amandio who stood in front of the rest. "Please my plane went down. My—" he paused in frustration, realizing they could not understand him.

"My friend…" Kane added, trying to continue. He could not stop thinking that Frost might still be alive, trying to swim ashore as he did. Frustrated, he stood up and shouted, demanding to speak with the man in charge. However, he was no longer in America. The man in charge was the one who now lifted a fully loaded AK-47 to his trigger finger, because of Kane's sudden outburst. Amandio did not know what to make of Kane's brave spasm. He yanked him by his striped-colored Puma shirt and dragged him away from the shore.

He tossed Kane against the palm tree. His back slammed against the bottom, nearly taking his breath. He knew now to keep quiet. Kane took a better look at the soldiers. They all looked too young to be policemen, or soldiers for that matter. He took mental notes, glancing at all of them, including Kweku and his cousin. He noticed that the pair were not armed and were kept at a distance from the rest of Amandio's men.

"Beautiful," said one of Amandio's men, stripping Kane of his gold-link chain, along with his over-sized pendant. Kane grimaced—lowering his head in disappointment. He knew things were taking a bad turn. Kane watched as Amandio's rugged hands wrapped around his wrist, clearing his gold nugget bracelet. It took no more than two minutes before he was cleaned of most of his possessions. His socks and jeans remained; they were useless to the undersized menaces. Kane was tall; an inch or so shorter than the lengthy Kweku. The soldiers sat under the mango tree for hours entertaining themselves with Kane's jewelry.

Kweku and Kgosi watched impatiently without humor. Kgosi was still amazed by Kane's presence and kept his eyes on him. He was sure Kane was royalty. It was the jewelry perhaps, coupled with Kane's mysterious entrance into Africa. Kgosi was growing more agitated by each taunt delivered by Amandio's brainless crew. He honestly felt they were mistreating a king.

Kweku on the other hand, was thinking that Kane made the perfect distraction. He made their escape much easier. *We'll leave tonight before they kill him.* Kweku was detached from the entire spectacle. *This is unfortunate, but this entire war was unfortunate,* thought Kweku as he watched Amandio strut around sporting Kane's gold pedant.

*What fools.* Kweku sighed to himself, and they were the worst kind; ones that would kill and rape in an instant. Kweku had first-hand knowledge of their type. He knew his own death would come shortly if he didn't escape soon.

Kane fought off the oversized mosquitoes circling the palm tree. His stomach grew tight. He was hungry, and after being planted against the tree for hours, he had begun to lose feeling in his legs. *How much longer can they carry on like this,* Kweku thought to himself. He thought about Kane. As soon as they became bored with him, Kweku was certain Amandio would chop Kane into pieces with his rusty machete. Amandio was a trained soldier. There wasn't a chance in hell he was bringing Kane, a rich American, back to headquarters. It would cause a long line of questions. Kane was as good as dead. His jewelry and clothes were saving his life for the moment.

"Look, Kgosi, we are leaving tonight," Kweku whispered in their native tongue, ensuring total secrecy.

"And the king?" Kgosi questioned quietly as he watched Amandio's men dance around with Kane's jewelry.

"He's no king, cousin. He is just a lost man." Kweku ran down his plan for later that night.

Kgosi protested. "Kweku! I will not leave this man!"

"I won't fight with you, he's your problem. Not mine." Kweku was frustrated by Kgosi's outrageous theory.

———

Meanwhile, back at Miami International Airport.

A press area was set up inside the Air Traffic Control conference room.

"Okay, they've been waiting for over an hour now," said Jim Warner, Commander and Team Leader of the Control Station. He headed down the elevator with some FBI and FAA folks. The press conference was nearly an hour past due.

Cameras flashed uncontrollably as Jim made his way to the podium. He had just returned from vacation in the Bahamas and wished he was still there playing with his two-year old. All the major news media outlets in the country had their microphones fixed on top of the stand.

"Good afternoon," Jim Warner said, his blue eyes mere slits. "It is confirmed that yesterday's flight 9098, which took off from Miami International bound for Rio de Janeiro, Brazil, crash landed some miles off the coast of Brazil into the Atlantic Ocean. The Brazilian government has already deployed a search and rescue team. An American ship will be heading to the area within the next five hours." Jim, at the FBI's request, did not mention how close the plane actually was to the coast of Africa—Northern Angola, no less. Jim continued uninterrupted, "There were eight people aboard: Tom Wilson, the captain; Ted Keene, the co-pilot, Tameka Moore, the flight-attendant; the traveling passengers were Kane C. Davis, Gabriel de Santos Fernando, Robert Dane, Julie Rivera and Emanuel Wright. At this time, we cannot confirm any causalities or survivors. Any questions?" Jim pointed to a reporter on the left side.

After a long thirty minutes most of the important questions were answered as vaguely as the FBI would have wanted. Kane's plane went down less than ten miles from a major airport in Luanda. If they had been flying slightly higher, they would have been blown out of the sky by Angolan forces.

—

Back in Northern Angola.

The sun had gone down. Kweku and Kgosi thought only of their escape now. Three hours ago, it became clear that Amandio and his goons were not planning to move from this spot anytime soon. They had all the mangoes they could ever want, and after three straight weeks in the forest eating practically nothing, this tree was not easy to leave behind.

In the morning, they would start making their way up north, back to the command station. Kweku knew they would have a lighter load for their trip. They would be killed either tonight or in the morning, and it would happen suddenly. The same fate awaited Kane. They'd keep his jewelry and free themselves of his clothes to avoid suspicion.

Kane was positioned awkwardly against a tree the entire time, his legs numb. He could not believe his predicament. He thought to himself, *what are the odds of crash landing off the coast of Brazil near the jungle and being surrounded by soldiers, intent on breaking every law in the book?* He spent his time watching all of them. Kweku and his cousin confused Kane the most. They were different and seemed to share the same dislike for Amandio. Kane amused himself by taking mental notes of who was the most misbehaved soldier for his verbal report to their captain. He was clueless about the level of danger he had stumbled upon.

Kgosi kept a firm eye on Kane after confirming the plan of escape with Kweku. They were leaving as soon as Kweku gave the signal. Kgosi pondered for hours, trying to figure out how to gain Kane's trust. He was nearly out of time. If only Kane knew a dialect of Kimbundu or even Portuguese, Kgosi could explain the eminent danger he was in. His life could end at any moment. The only warning offered would be a smirk or a grin from Amandio, then it would all be over.

"Your name?" Kgosi asked in a deep whisper, inching over in Kane's direction. Amandio and the others were asleep, but one of his men was ordered to watch them closely. The watchman had been carefully placed behind the three of them, but even his eyes were wearing thin. Kgosi inched closer to Kane. Kane turned sharply, unaware of the necessity for silence. He gazed at Kgosi in confusion. At that moment, Kgosi felt that befriending Kane would be nearly impossible, but then the word that may save Kane's fragile existence "amigo," was whispered. Kgosi was trying desperately to show Kane that he was someone he could trust. He softly placed his hand on his chest, and repeated, "amigo," giving Kane a genuine smile full of bright, white teeth.

Kane immediately understood and relaxed his constricted face. Kgosi and Kweku were on his side. He'd heard the word "amigo" in the Bronx a million times. Frost always used it in an attempt to calm down some irate customer.

Kgosi was relieved to see that Kane understood. He returned to his spot. Kweku stared at Kgosi in frustration. *We cannot die for this stranger,* Kweku thought to himself. Akua, his love, meant more to him than anything—perhaps even more than the beliefs of the village. However, his cousin remained committed to those beliefs, especially about brotherhood and love.

An hour passed and the watchman's eyes weakened with every minute. Even Kane had grown sleepy from this unimaginable day. Kweku's eyes continuously circled the terrain—planning, plotting, and looking for the right moment. It was now. Amandio was sound asleep. The mosquitoes were feasting on his flesh and yet he did not move an inch. *If the watch had been left to Amandio, they could have escaped a long time ago.* The moment came upon them. They needed to leave now or they would more than likely be shot in the morning.

"Bathroom," Kweku called out to the watchman in a careful tone. He didn't want to wake the others. The watchman, slightly startled by Kweku's voice, quickly readied his rifle and took aim at Kweku's head. "The bathroom?" Kweku asked again, quickly lifting his empty hands. Annoyed by the surprise, the watchman stared at Kweku, keeping aim at his head longer than normal. "Let's go," the weary soldier nearly shouted. Praying the loud voice did not disturb the others, Kweku looked around anxiously. Lucky for them, Amandio hated the smell of urine or human waste, so everyone was allowed to go relieve themselves, if accompanied of course. Kweku's plan was working so far.

Kgosi eyed Kweku as he passed. Kweku gave the sign by widening his eyes, signaling a wrath of things to follow. Unlike Kweku's careful nerves, a sharp chill crept up Kgosi's spine. He cautiously turned toward Kane's slumbering body. He moved over to signal him.

"Go here," the watchman shoved his rifle into Kweku's left side. He found a tree about forty feet from Amandio and the rest of his men. Privacy was a luxury. The watchman stood directly behind him. Kweku took one last look at the position of the watchman's rifle and turned his back to urinate. The soldier's rifle was carelessly pointed to the ground, perfect for Kweku.

Kweku went for his zipper.

Suddenly, in one swift motion, Kweku threw himself back, plunging the back of his head into the watchman's nose. He wrapped his long fingers neatly around the front end of the rifle and pulled it away. Thick blood poured from the watchman's disorganized nose, as he dropped back to cover his face.

Kgosi glanced over and saw their boots pressed against rubble. The watchman reached for Kweku's neck, but grasped his face. His attempt to stop the overgrown Angolan had failed, Kweku's strength was unbearable.

He shoved the watchman's body against the tree and began choking the life from him with the rifle.

The struggle continued, Kweku tried to keep it quiet and did. Kweku searched the man's face, waiting for his eyes to roll back. After forty long seconds, they finally did. The watchman's grip on Kweku's face began to loosen. Kweku lifted him up and snapped his neck, assuring he was dead. Kgosi, watched in shock. Kweku thought of killing the rest of them, but they were too spread out. It was too risky.

Kgosi sharply tugged at Kane's leg. It took only one jerk to wake him. Kane had always been a light sleeper. "Let's go!" Kgosi said to Kane, whispering and pointing in the direction of the struggle. Kane's stomach weakened, as he glanced over and saw Kweku quietly placing the limp body off to one side of the tree; his hands and arms covered in blood.

In that moment, he began to realize the danger of the situation. He tried desperately not to panic as Kgosi clutched his right arm. He guided him away into the darkest part of the forest, behind Kweku. So far, the plan had been executed with perfection. Kgosi was troubled by Kweku's quick and silent murder of the watchman. Kweku was changing. His heart was becoming colder and colder with each kill. Kweku did not give the murder another thought as they crept together, heading for the heart of the forest.

## Chapter Fifteen

THEY'D BEEN RUNNING FOR HOURS. Kweku had wisely chosen a different route. They were running south, trying to throw off Amandio. Going east, back towards their village was an obvious choice so they continued in the opposite direction. Kweku did not want to lead Amandio to his village. Amandio was ruthless, and he was no stranger to the terrain or to the war. Kweku did not want to take any chances with Kane in tow—at least not yet.

"Please," Kane begged, nearly out of breath. He had no shoes, and his feet were numb from the prickly ground of the forest. He needed to grab Kgosi's attention. He needed rest.

He stumbled over a broken branch and fell to his knees.

He lifted his head, but was too exhausted to stand. He lied on the ground, gasping.

Kweku turned back. "What is it now?" He asked in his native tongue. It was just the two of them and Kane—no need for Portuguese.

"Let's rest, cousin. He needs rest," Kgosi said, coming to Kane's aid.

"We've rested enough," Kweku responded, unaware of Kane's traumatic twenty-four hours. Kweku parked himself in frustration next to a nearby tree.

Kgosi gently helped Kane into a sitting position. The forest filled his ears with strange noises, forcing Kane to flinch frantically. He leaned back against the base of a tree, trying to collect his breath. He tried to make sense of everything. Tears softly trickled down from his right eye. He tried to hold them back, but the misery of the day forced them out quietly. He remained silent, thinking of the plane crash—about Frost and Roxy dying in front of him. And now, running through the forest with armed strangers, one of whom clearly did not care much for him. He coiled up to the tree like a child. In spite of Kgosi and Kweku's presence, Kane crumbled and a light sob began to surface. He started to whimper. Kweku looked on without care, thinking only of how much of a liability Kane had become.

Kgosi gently embraced Kane's left shoulder and remained silent. He knew this was no place for tears, but Kane was different to him.

"So much for your king," Kweku said, standing up. He was fully irritated as he continued to watch Kane snivel.

"I'm going to look for food. Stay put," he instructed, bringing his rifle to a ready position. It was easy to get distracted by all that had transpired over the past twenty-four hours, but Kweku never forgot that they were knee-deep in a nasty war. Death could be moments away. He understood this, and knew that his home inside his village was the only safe place.

Kane finally began to calm down as a hint of sunrise emerged through the cracks of the densely covered branches. The forest was frightening, especially at night. It seemed that all of the wildlife in the jungle awoke, carrying sounds of thirst and danger—echoes all too familiar to Kgosi and Kweku. They'd spent their lives listening to them, but Kane's fresh ears flinched at every sound.

"My name," Kgosi said, placing his hand on his chest and continuing, "Kgosi." He repeated again, "Kgosi."

"Your name?" Kgosi directed his finger to Kane's knee. Kane said, "Kane," happy to understand something. He repeated it again with a half smile, "Kane."

"Brazil?" Kane asked, pointing to the ground.

"Brazil?" Kgosi responded, partially confused, "Ah, no. Africa. Angola," Kgosi explained.

Kane's heart dropped. "Africa!" Kane yelled. After getting the head nod of confirmation from Kgosi, he collapsed against the tree into a hopeless sigh.

*Africa?*

*Angola?*

Egypt was the only African country he could locate on a map. The war had not received a lot of press in the States; not that Kane would have known it anyway. In school, he thought geography was a waste of time.

He looked at Kgosi, trying to fight off his distress. He knew Kgosi was handling him with special care, but he did not know why. He stared at the top of the forest in anguish, trying to collect some hope.

Meanwhile, Kweku probed through the forest.

He eyed a deep opening ahead where there were no more trees. He had reached the edge of the forest. Kweku, curious, headed towards the opening.

"Lights?" He questioned, walking pass the last tree in the forest. He stood out of the forest and looked on in amazement. There were small lights sprinkled across the earth in the distance. His uncle had explained this lighting phenomenon to the village several times, but it was nothing like seeing it for the first time, especially off in a distance. It was the first town Kweku had ever seen like it. Remembering his uncle's stories, he knew they had a better chance of finding food there than in the unforgiving forest. Kweku jogged back for the others, invigorated.

Meanwhile, near the shore, almost forty miles away.

"Amandio!" shouted one of the soldiers who discovered the watchman's battered body. It was blanketed with bugs. Kweku left the solider bleeding profusely from his face. The blood attracted some small forest animals, which left his arm and face nearly stripped to the bone.

Gruesome.

Amandio unstartled by the soldier's rant, got up slowly, still shaking off sleep. Soldiers rarely slept well out in the forest. They were in constant battle with mosquitoes and the endless rattles and howls of the forest. However, Amandio, for whatever reason, always managed to sleep soundly.

He finally made it over.

"Nelson," Amandio whispered, quietly hovering over the wretched body. "Brother," he said. The dead soldier was Amandio's half brother. They had the same mother. He kept it secret during the war, afraid that someone would use it to get leverage over him. Backing away from his brother's battered body; he slipped into a dark rage and snatched his rifle from one of his subjects.

They all stood ready; faces red with fury. He stared down his circle of soldiers. His eyes were cold, filled with regret and vengeance. *I should have killed him a long time ago,* Amandio thought to himself. He flung the broken radio against the tree. There was no doubt he was headed back into the forest. He was not interested in winning this war, anyhow. In fact, he joined it only to be armed and, after his first clutch of the AK-47, it was bad news for over two hundred Africans. After a while, he killed people from his own town. Between making sure that his belly was full and getting into a few gun fights, Amandio's life had been empty—until now. Now, it had a purpose. "Let's go!" Amandio violently snatched Kane's chain from the soldier's neck. He was no stranger to the forest, but Kweku's cleverness had worked for the moment. Amandio and his team headed east while Kweku was still traveling south.

Forty miles south of Amandio's fury.

Kweku suddenly appeared from the trees, giving Kgosi a soft scare.

"I found something. Let's go," Kweku instructed. He had always kept things short, even when he was commanding his unit. Kgosi never questioned Kweku's authority. Although back home in the village, Kweku's words were normally quiet and soft. It took Kgosi some time to adjust to Kweku's new demeanor, but he understood why. The war was sure to change people and it was changing Kweku by the hour.

Wearily collecting himself from the tree, Kane began his uncoordinated stride behind Kgosi. His feet were battered from the long run. They'd gone forty miles in eight hours without water, but he had to press on. He had no choice. Now that he knew he was in Africa, he knew to keep quiet and humble about things, but his thirst was unbearable. He was down to his last bit of energy. He looked back at his cozy spot against the tree, thinking that maybe it would be a good place to die.

"Let's go," Kgosi said, softly pulling at Kane's right arm. He lowered his head and followed behind the anxious Kweku.

They'd been speed walking for twenty minutes and Kgosi was increasingly concerned as Kane's stride became weaker and weaker. They fell further behind.

"What is it cousin? Where are we going?" Kgosi wanted them to rest then head back to the village, especially carrying Kane. They were vulnerable with him.

"It's a village, Kgosi, with electricity—the lights your father spoke of." Kweku was annoyed by all the questions and by the lingering American.

"Electricity?" Kgosi asked, confused.

Kweku continued a strong, steady walk through the edge of the forest, ignoring the both of them.

"*Finally,*" Kweku said to himself, exhausted. *Maybe there's water here.* The sky was white from the might of the sun. Finally, it was morning. They all made their first steps out of the forest. The lights to the town were gone, but it was clear a township existed, as small yellow brick homes where exposed through the green of the tall bushes. Kweku, held his smile back, but was happy he had not imagined the whole thing.

With every step, Kane's slouch deepened from the weight of the sun. It was surprising he had made it out of the forest. The heat seemed to be a greater enemy than any army brigade that might be scattered throughout the country.

Unable to endure another step, Kane fell to his knees. His plummet to the dry, dusty soil, grabbed even Kweku's attention. Kane's dry face crashed to the earth.

"Kweku!" Kgosi called out in a panic. Irritated with Kgosi, Kweku marched back to the fallen body and swept Kane from the ground in one motion. Kweku's strength was astonishing. He had not eaten or had anything to drink in nearly two days, but he was able to carry Kane's 210-pound body over his shoulder for another three miles.

As they got closer to the township, the beauty, which existed from a far, began to waste away. The small, yellow brick, one-story villas were filled with bullet holes. The roofs, once carefully covered with sheet metal, were tattered and quickly patched. Kweku noticed there were more birds than usual hovering over—most likely looking for dead flesh.

It was soulless. Empty. The aftermath of a vicious shootout. It was once a thriving township—the ones Kgosi's father had spoken of.

After passing the first villa, Kweku looked up the hill at a few carefully painted three and four-story buildings. *Please let there be water there,* Kweku pleaded in silence. In the back of Kweku's mind, Kane's condition was troubling him, although he would never admit it to Kgosi. He knew water could be in the township, but it was most likely not safe to drink. With the amount of shell casings scattered around, bodies were not far away. Kweku hoped he could avoid seeing them. They made their way forward to the peach-colored building Kweku pointed out.

"Trouble makers, trouble makers," three kids ran pass them yelling in their native Nganguela tongue. Kweku's AK-47 and army uniform had invited the outburst. Kweku lived too far away to understand what it meant. For a moment, he'd forgotten the war. Secretly, he was more worried about Kane's health, which seemed to be deteriorating fast.

The town was nearly deserted. It seemed to have fallen victim to countless clashes, leaving many of the buildings partially collapsed, mainly from tank fire. The war had spilled into this town, which was once a thriving, White, middle-class community. Most of the Whites left years ago, when the war first began. However, running water still existed in some small towns and big cities, including this one.

The more affluent Whites had once populated this part of the town. It once was a quiet, suburban town filled with doctors, businessmen, and lawyers. It rested in a great location, with an astonishing view of a plush green forest overlaid with majestic mountains from the highlands. One of the more welcomed scenes around the country. Long ago, it was a sacred place for the Nganguela tribes, but when the Portuguese penetrated the interior in 1650, the Nganguela tribes had been forced back some hundred miles. It was not until the 1940s that they had been allowed to build a Black township near this White town.

Kweku studied the area as he rested Kane's limp body in the shade. They had stopped at an abandoned petrol station to plan their next move. Kgosi watched over Kane anxiously. Kane looked like just another Angolan who had been swallowed into the breast of this brutal war.

"Wait here," Kweku said, forgetting everything. He paraded into town with an AK-47, decorated in full military gear, nearly 150 miles away from headquarters. If there were soldiers from the other side present, he would have been shot dead. He noticed a small marketplace carefully set up in front of a dilapidated motel and headed over.

"Where is the water?" Kweku asked, making his dry mouth speak Portuguese first. Showing signs of fatigue, he stood over an old woman selling tebo nuts and cassava. The market was humble, maybe fifteen to twenty people in all, with eight vendors. *It seems so empty here.* Kweku thought to himself while he waited for an answer.

The people seemed to be few in numbers. She quickly pointed back to the petrol station.

A strange, older man made his way over. He seemed friendly enough. He was a local minister for what used to be the Black township Kweku had just passed. He softly explained that the water in the petrol station's bathroom was drinkable if you did not drink too much. If you drank too much, it would make you sick, but you would not die. The cheerful minister did not know what to make of Kweku at first. Was he a soldier lost from his group ready to stir up trouble? Then he saw Kweku's rifle carefully placed behind his back and breathed a sigh of relief.

The minister had learned to be extra polite to anyone in uniform, whatever the side—and especially to anyone carrying a rifle. But Kweku seemed different from the others. Maybe it was his politeness and his clear-spoken Portuguese. He felt comfortable around the oversized soldier.

"Come, come with me," Kweku said as the minister hurried— understanding the urgency. He matched Kweku's fast stride towards Kane's direction. The helpful minister rushed to Kane's feeble body. His situation seemed to have worsened. His face was scorched, dried out and his lips cracked, filled with dust. His arms and legs had cramped up as well, but he was too weak to respond. Instead, he laid there twitching in pain.

He seemed to be dying. Kgosi's face grieved as if Kane was his own brother. Kgosi tried to fix his emotions around the stranger, as he turned his head up. After giving Kane a look over, the minister was less alarmed about the situation and hurried to the bathroom. Kane was not in immediate danger. He was simply dehydrated. At most, he would pass out for an hour or so. He needed just a few liters of water and some rest, and then he would be good as new. The minister had seen much worse over the years.

Hours passed.

A hint of night crept over the empty town. Kweku and the others were taken to a church a few miles from the petrol station. The minister was outdoing himself. Kweku was slightly suspicious of his kindness, but was happy to accept it. After it was confirmed that Kane would live, Kweku returned to his sharp senses, examining everything in sight. They all gathered in the sleeping quarters downstairs.

The church seemed to have been the least damaged building in the town. There were only a few bullet holes in the front and along the sides. Many of the fighting men were catholic, which could explain why the church was not badly damaged; and perhaps the minister's kindness.

Some people were still alive and healthy, in a town where the only thing that seemed to work was scattered amounts of electricity and running water in a few places.

"What is your name?" The minister asked in a soft voice. With Kane and Kgosi tucked away in the next room asleep from all the excitement, Kweku was left to deal with the minister's inquiry.

"My name is Kweku," he said, happy to finally abandon his pseudonym Antonio. The minister seemed harmless enough. Besides, Kweku kept his AK-47 inches from his reach.

"You know, the men—the soldiers—will return," he added. The minister looked out the side window, suggesting Kane was on the opposite side of the rebel group hovering around the area. Kweku did not bother to respond. He did not intend to stay beyond tomorrow. He wanted to drop Kane off here, collect some provisions, and head northeast, back home to his village with Kgosi.

He turned to the minister. "This guy is sick. Can you help him? My cousin and I must leave him. He is a stranger here. You can help him better than we can." Kweku had had enough of Kane and of his cousin's growing affection for him. It was time to get home—back to the village. Ignoring the core belief of the village, he had no intension of bringing Kane back home.

"Stranger?" The minister asked, puzzled.

"Yes, he is an American, I believe. My cousin and I found him in the forest." Kweku quickly changed the story to protect himself. He really didn't want the attention and started to regret giving the minister his true name.

"An American soldier?" The minister asked, still baffled.

"Yes, I think maybe that's it," Kweku openly lied, wanting to drop the subject. He was really looking for a yes or no from the man.

"Okay, I can have him talk with the medical staff at the hospital. There are a few English-speaking doctors there from Australia. The chief medical doctor is Chinese, Dr. Chin, but he also speaks English." The minister ran down his plan as Kweku stood up, headed for the window.

The night was still young, and Kweku wanted to look around. He was still in military mode, and after the news from the minister, he was extra cautious about soldiers in the area.

He heard a few rocks fall off the top of a partially collapsed restaurant. He turned quickly. The night was dark. Silent. And the lights that had appeared so luminous from afar were dim—flickering off and on. Kweku eyed a partial silhouette standing behind the restaurant. It was a soldier, one of Sabovio's men, spying in on the church.

Sabovio commanded rebel armies from mostly the central part of the country. His army was vicious and could easily claim responsibility for much of the casualties in the war. They raided villages and towns in the interior of the country and used guerilla tactics in the larger cities

where their opposition had the upper hand. While they were danger-
ously disorganized in the beginning, they still managed to be taken
seriously by the northern army—the one in which Kweku and Kgosi
had belonged. They put a military strain on captured cities by using
short-range missiles and nightly raids. Many of the captured cities and
towns in the central and some northern parts of the country ended up
like this ghostly town.

Some Angolans considered Sabovio's rebels to be heroes, but most
considered them God's worst enemy. At one point they seemed to have
a legitimate cause—fighting for liberation, although now they were
aimless, fighting without any true purpose. It was said that Sabovio was
the most ruthless leader of all the armies. Worst of all, he was stationed
only thirty short miles outside this little town.

The soldier fell back behind the rubble, as Kweku strained his eyes
through the window for a closer look.

"What is it?" The minister asked, noticing Kweku's concern. For
now, the church was safe. There was a small NATO army patrolling
major parts of the city, but if Sabovio wanted to, he could retake the
city in one night. However, much of its population was dead so there
was no reason to. Kweku's presence; however, could be just the
motivation Sabovio needed for a gunfight. That is why the minister
wanted them off the street; the town was crawling with snitches.

"You should get some sleep," the minister said, sensing Kweku's
weariness. They had traveled nearly fifty miles today, with no food or
water. However, sleep would have to wait. Kweku was not closing his
eyes until he had scoped everything out first. He was always careful.
Back home in the village, he had looked out into the forest for hours
after Akua's father had been killed by that leopard, hoping to avenge his

uncle's death. "I will look around for a while, and then I'll rest," Kweku said, leaving the window as he made for his rifle.

The church was old. It had been rebuilt in the late 1800s. The builders had tried to keep the colonial style, using window frames of Mary, Christ, and Joseph that dated back to the 1500s. Although the windows were shattered, pieces of Mary's face remained, staring down at everyone who passed through the main hall. The church was beautiful and well-kept, considering the condition of the rest of the town. Kweku continued his exploration, poking his readied gun into every dark spot around the antiquated place.

As much as Kgosi disapproved of Kweku's growing rudeness, he was happy to have him. He had proven himself worthy of his cousin, Akua; perhaps even before they left the village. Although his younger cousin Kirabo died under his watch, being bitten by a deadly bug is unavoidable.

Kweku heard the sound of running water coming from the study rooms on the second level. A slight rush of energy flooded his belly. He tightened his grip on the rifle. The minister said there was no one else inside the church.

*It was too good to be true, staying here for the night,* he thought. He contemplated running back for the others, but thought he should confirm the ambush first. He crept slowly up the old wooden steps. Each step made a different noise. *Hopefully the running water will conceal the squeaky racket,* he thought.

The hall upstairs was long, dark, and overly narrow. The intruder had nowhere to run, except in his direction. Kweku hesitated. It took him nearly twenty seconds before he could summon the courage to take his first step down the eerie passageway. The moonlight covered his first steps, but the further he walked down the hall, the darker it became. A small bead of sweat trickled down the right side of his cheek.

The trigger on his rifle moistened from his grip.

His nerves on edge.

Cowardly men would have discharged their weapon before entering, but Kweku, although showing obvious signs of fear, managed to control it.

The sound of water grew louder.

He heard it hitting the floor

Only a few feet away now.

He readied his rifled and reached for the door, but it was already cracked open.

Using the nose of the rifle, he quietly pushed it in further. It was a bathroom. A hue of midnight blue covered the entire room—it streamed in from the broken window.

Kweku got ready to fire.

His moistened index finger applied pressure on the trigger.

He opened the door fully, and then quickly removed his finger from the trigger.

*A girl!* He gasped quietly. He put his rifle to the ground. She was strikingly beautiful. She looked to be about eighteen and stood naked with her back turned away from him. She did not yet realize he was just fifteen feet away. She continued washing her unblemished skin in the back sink.

Kweku noticed a broken urinal affixed to the sidewall. The room was once a men's bathroom. Her long sleek body reminded him of Akua. Kweku stood watching her, thinking of how he and Akua would sneak out and watch lovers beneath the waterfall. Running sink water from the battered town was a far cry from a natural spring, but it was the sound it made that kept Kweku daydreaming quietly.

She aroused him.

He stood there sighing softly.

Suddenly, the rifle accidentally hit the door. She turned quickly, dropping the wash pail. Water ran across the floor.

"Sorry," Kweku said softly. He had not yet realized that when wearing an army fatigue and carrying a loaded AK-47, he did not need to be polite - but he still was. She was startled but surprisingly unafraid. She was the minister's daughter. He kept her out of sight. She rarely left the church, and if she did, she was accompanied at all times. Filled with fresh beauty, she stood there uncovered, allowing Kweku to continue gazing at her shapely figure.

Kweku felt a bit awkward. He had never had sex before and had no interest in foreplay. His body wanted to grab her by the hair and make violent love to her on the bathroom floor. He had plenty of opportunities back home, but he wanted to wait for Akua. But now, knee-deep in this war, he knew there was a good chance that he'd never see her again. He thought through all of this while remaining fixed at the door.

She stared him down, waiting. It was clear what she wanted. She was exhausted from her father's never-ending quest to keep her hidden. And with her hormones raging, she was ready to sleep with anyone. Puzzled by Kweku's reluctance to pounce on her, she smiled softly and held out her left arm for his taking. Kweku slowly made his way over. He gasped as their faces met closely. She was even more beautiful than he thought. Her light brown eyes were unusual, strange to him, exotic. Her teeth were bright white, like his. She was a beauty, and Kweku had trouble resisting.

Despite the drama he'd endured over the past few weeks, Kweku was still a very handsome man. Studying his tall, lean body through the green army uniform, she suddenly pulled him in towards her. She found her eyes looking up at the stunning nineteen year old. They made a nice couple.

She smirked then grabbed his belt.

Kweku was in a trance until he heard his belt becoming unfixed. He jerked back, thinking of Akua and the promise to himself. *I would rather die a virgin than make love to another.* Kweku gently refastened his belt buckle. Their eyes met in total silence, his telling the entire story without muttering a word. She left, still wet, slowly walking pass him, and then headed down the dark of the hallway.

Kweku turned the water off and parked himself on top of the sink, staring out the window. He spoke aloud, "Akua, I miss you. I hope you are well. If I don't return, find me in the wind." Kweku found a cozy place to sleep against the wall in the bathroom.

The night loosened its grip as a hint of sunlight peeked over the horizon. It was morning.

Singing vibrated the walls of the church.

Somewhere between heaven and earth lied the unwavering call to God every Sunday. What was left of this worn-out town gathered in harmonious sounds too beautiful to describe. The song repeated, awakening Kane, who was now somewhat energized from his long sleep. They nursed him back with fresh nuts, cassava, yams, beef stew and loads of water. Still very far from his normal life, but the hymns rising up from the church helped him forget the last twenty-four hours for a moment. He remained fixed to the thin mat, quietly listening.

The singing seemed to explain everything: the endless fighting, slavery, the exploitation, and the emptiness of the country. There were once happy songs sung in the neighboring township, but now they sang pleading with God to spare the country and to spare themselves of misery, but not death. Kane continued listening and the hymns moved him, even though he did not understand a word.

The door opened and the minister entered.

"How are things?" The minister, smiling, asked Kgosi. The war had claimed most of his family. He was left guarding his oldest daughter and his wife's mother. The rest of his family had been killed two years ago. He was a devout Catholic, who placed all his cares in the hands of God. He was a kind, loving man. It would have been difficult, even for a drunken soldier to justify killing him. Although he was somewhat protected by the NATO army and was considered a great friend to many of the foreign agencies centered in the main part of the town, he still took few risks. He knew how easily someone could be killed by a wandering rebel.

"I am well, thank you." Kgosi was always polite. It was the way of Angolans to show deep respect to their elders, although teenagers Kgosi's age had lost that concept since the war began. Kgosi's strict adherence to traditions and kind heart at such a young age was unique. He had the patience of a God and even showed great courage during the gunfight some weeks back. He would make a great king someday.

"The American. I know people who speak his language. English. They are doctors from the hospital. They can help him," the minister explained, giving Kgosi the good news. It's a shame Kane couldn't make out the minister's words, he would have been delighted.

"That is good news!" Kgosi said, smiling as he looked across at Kane. The minister addressed Kane with the little English he'd picked up from the Australian doctor. "Hello. My name is Alfonso Mukenga. I am minister here." The minister tapped Kane's left shoulder, eager to challenge his English. With each word released from the minister's mouth—however strained—Kane sighed in relief. He turned over and broke into an exhausting half smile.

"Can you help me?" Kane asked humbly. Based on his earlier experience with Amandio, he knew not to demand anything. It was the softest request of his life.

"Yes, they have men here. They will speak English for you." The minister reached out his hand to Kane.

Kane could not help but believe that God was personally protecting him. First escaping death with Keys, the plane crash and then meeting Kgosi and Kweku. Without them, he was good as dead in the hands of Amandio. Now this. In the middle of a brutal war, he finds help that will most likely land him home.

He put his hands together, thanking God silently. In all the years attending the Kingdom Hall, Jehovah Witness Church, he had never believed in God as much as he did at that moment.

"Come, let's go, my friends!" The minister guided Kane and Kgosi to the music.

Meanwhile, a mere thirty miles outside the town at Sabovio's camping ground.

"General," the spy Kweku spotted from last night reported back, out of breath. Fear and loyalty gave him the strength to sprint nearly thirty miles without stopping. Sabovio was the leader of his army. Although they referred to him as general, he was the political leader as well. He loosely took orders from the South African Army, when it suited him. He commanded what would be considered five large brigades with a soldier count perhaps in the tens of thousands.

"There are three soldiers in town with uniforms and rifles." The spy bent down exhausted.

"Soldiers?" Sabovio stood up and walked pass two of his most trusted generals. He made his way to the front to talk to the worn out spy.

Sabovio was a midsize man in his forties with a hardened face. Over the years he may have personally killed over 5,000 combatants belonging to the Northern Army, something he spoke of proudly. The older soldiers feared him, while most of the younger ones honored and praised him.

Surprisingly, he was willing to speak openly about the war. Some thought he spoke too much to be a leader, but he'd easily back his words with action. However, wisely, he did try to avoid conventional gunfights. Most of his soldiers were not trained for war and were not capable of holding a front line; mainly due to fear and inexperience. Nonetheless, with ties to the South African army and funding overseas, he remained a long-standing threat in the war, leaving the African citizens of Angola to endure much of the suffering.

Sabovio's army was a unique threat in other ways—landmines. His army was responsible for setting over four million of them over an eight-year period. One of his objectives was to destabilize a city that had been captured by the opposition. They were able to weaken the security of these cities by placing landmines everywhere. They killed and mutilated thousands—mostly the innocent. Like most of the armies, he ultimately wanted to press northward to Luanda.

"Yes, sir," the spy said, avoiding eye contact out of fear and respect. Soldiers rarely maintained steady eye contact with him, except for his generals, and even they were, at times, uneasy about his presence.

"Which direction did they come from?" One general asked.

The spy didn't know, but explained they most likely came from the north, which meant they were most likely enemies. Sabovio had two large platoons stationed a few miles west of this city but nothing north. Sabovio was very reactionary and emotional. He was not a great thinker; instead, his generals did most of his strategic planning.

"Okay," Sabovio said, gesturing the spy away. "I think we should..." one general started in on his opinion, but was quickly interrupted by Sabovio.

"We will go tonight. They are sending spies in to check the area. We will go after the sun goes down. Tell the spy to return to the city and report back to here before the sun is gone." For the first time, he didn't want to react immediately. Normally, he would have sent a few soldiers to collect Kweku and the others, but he thought the northern armies were close by and didn't want to give away key positions. It was a cautious move.

"We'll strike after the sun. Get your men ready!' Sabovio commanded. He ordered all his platoons east and west of the town to be on high alert. He even radioed the potential threat into the South African army.

All this drama swung into place over two cousins and one frightened American.

Back in town, the sun was blazing at full strength. It was nearly noon. After four hours, the singing had stopped and Kane seized his opportunity to speak with the Canadian doctor.

"Hi, my name is Kane Davis. My plane crashed landed here. We were trying to get to Brazil and…" Kane launched into his story, talking a mile a minute.

"Wait. What?" The Canadian asked, shocked and confused. "Wait, who are you?"

Kane took a breath and gave a slower version of his story. He even had his passport with him to prove it. Amandio and his goons were too distracted by his gold chains; they did not bother to check his pockets. Without his passport, his story would have been too incredible to believe. As it was, he was standing in the heart of Angola with over three platoons closing in on him in less than seven hours.

"I can't…I can't believe this," the doctors said, astonished. They were not sure if they were more surprised about the story or that he had not been killed by now. After what they'd heard broadcasted over the radio, it seemed that most of the country was swallowed in sporadic gunfights. This town was considered a safe zone. It had not seen any real action in a few months.

The doctors, themselves, just arrived a few months ago. With the UN under pressure, a small NATO battalion and a handful of doctors and engineers had been placed across the major cities and towns throughout the country. In this town of a meager thirty soldiers, Sabovio did not mind the presence of the UN. He knew if deemed necessary, his army could run over the town.

Kane's story was compelling. The doctors were still muttering in disbelief. Eventually, she said, "There is a NATO command station some miles away. We can take you up there after our shift tonight." The Canadian doctor had been impressed with Kane's humbleness. He agreed to everything and did not make a fuss about the wait. A mere twenty-four hours in Africa had clearly tamed him. He was petrified, and Kweku knew it. He looked on nearly forty yards away and could sense Kane pleading to the doctors. He stood around them as if their mere presence could protect him, forgetting for a moment that Kweku and Kgosi saved his life. He was too scared to remember anything. All he could think of now was going home.

"Hello," Kgosi said, always warm and polite, approaching the doctor. Kweku watched the exchange in disgust. "Can you translate for me?" Kgosi asked the doctor in Portuguese.

The doctor's Portuguese was impeccable. She had studied the language in Sao Paulo, Brazil for two years and had been speaking it for twelve. It helps when your husband is Brazilian as well. She finished her doctorate at the Northern Ontario School of Medicine and left Canada. She had never looked back. She joined the UN as a general medical doctor and was now able to speak four languages. She'd been on several humanitarian assignments, but said this was the worst, because it seemed that the world had turned their backs on the country. She always thought that everyone in Angola could be killed and no one would stop it.

"Yes, of course. And what's your name?" She asked, immediately picking up Kgosi's good Portuguese. Kgosi excitedly revealed everything. "My name is Kgosi. My cousin and I, live between the mountains you see there." Kgosi proudly pointed across to the mountains. "Tell him that I am very happy to meet him." Kgosi continued, still humble and overly friendly. "And tell him that my life is his." Kgosi made a strong gesture by placing a fist to his chest.

Kane was still puzzled by Kgosi's thick kindness. "Thank you. Thank You," Kane said. Although it was a genuine thank you, Kgosi did not receive the connection he was looking for.

"We need to get back," the doctor said, referring to the hospital. Mr. Mukenga had convinced nearly the entire medical staff to come out to sing on Sundays, but they needed to get back now. Even when they were present, the hospital was understaffed.

"Will you stay here?" The doctor asked, directing her question at Kane. "No. No. I'm going with you. I'll go to the hospital," Kane said anxiously. He found much more comfort in an English-speaking person. Being with her made him feel closer to home.

"Good-bye," Kane said, gesturing haphazardly to Kgosi and the others. He really wanted to go home, and who could blame him. He had nearly died in a horrific plane crash. He'd watched Kweku kill a soldier and he'd seen more than a handful of amputees from landmines, mostly children in the few blocks he traveled around town. Not to mention, he nearly died of dehydration yesterday. He was drenched in fear and carried an air that maybe his life was more valuable than everyone else's. It sickened Kweku. He sensed Kane's arrogance the moment he came ashore.

Kgosi was surprised by Kane's eagerness to leave. *There's so much I want to tell him about me and about our village.* His excited childlike feelings towards Kane broke into an awkward numbness as Kane waved a short goodbye from the jeep.

⟶

Hours had passed.

Sabovio and his generals quickly prepared for a full-scale attack. They had unofficial control over this province for nearly a full year. If the northern opposition took it, it could collapse their stronghold on much of the interior. It was an important location for them, mainly because of the water. The entire rebel force knew what was at stake. Sabovio and his rebels were overmatched conventionally. Their fighting tactics always resulted in nasty guerrilla attacks, expelling forces in hidden locations, and taking aim at anyone who was suspicious. This approach resulted in soldiers shooting at innocent people. Innocent life was never a priority for either side.

Twenty jeeps, jammed-packed with soldiers heavily armed with RPGs and AK-47s, pulled up in front of the generals west of the city. Their wheels were covered in mud. "We're ready," the commander said, jumping down from the jeep—and they were. Eventually there would be nearly eight hundred heavily armed soldiers ready to retake a city already in their control from both sides. Sabovio's command was all that separated this already battered town from yet another vicious gun clash. The NATO army would be no match for them. And, with the Northern army nowhere in sight, this was a pending disaster for the town. Kweku and his two-man crew now drew the attention of the entire UNDA rebel force and central headquarters of the South African army.

Meanwhile, back at the hospital.

Kane tried desperately to find a place to escape the hospital traffic. It told the full story of the bleak suffering of the Angolan people. Most of the patients who entered the hospital came here because of the war. But, so many were simply tragic victims of the lack of security, leading to a level of violence so overwhelming that most of the doctors constantly wondered if, when they left, would they have made a difference at all. With nowhere to go, Kane parked himself on the steps near the side entrance and watched all the people, most of whom were women and children, entering and exiting the hospital. Streaks of dried and fresh blood stained the entrance of the hospital. In the States, a bloody entrance would have drawn numerous complaints, but here in Angola, an unkempt entrance was the least of their problems.

"Chibinda, chibinda (hunter, hunter)," a young boy greeted Kane with respect as he continued his approach to the weary American. Aside from his freshly faded haircut, Kane passed for Angolan. He'd been greeted several times in both Portuguese and Kimbundu. He got into the habit of ignoring it or simply nodding his head. He sensed this boy was going to be persistent; kids usually are.

His name was Ngosi—an eight-year-old boy, who had taken a pair of bullets to his face during a gunfight nearly a year ago. His face was a troubling sight. His left jaw and cheekbone were shattered, leaving his face horribly disfigured. Orphaned at two years old when his entire family had been killed by the rebel forces, he was left with nowhere to go after surgery. The hospital staff was happy to keep him around. With all the misery the war brought, Ngosi had an unnatural will to remain upbeat every day. The medical staff welcomed any happiness they could get. Many of the cases coming to the hospital were life and death, and most of them resulted in death.

Kane reluctantly waved at him, failing to notice Ngosi's left side. Kane was in his own world of shock and spiraling nerves; a nervousness that even he realized needed to come under control.

"Amigo," said Ngosi, again attempting to grab Kane's attention in Portuguese now.

"Hello," Kane said, finally looking up and taking notice. Although he'd seen many horrible things sitting outside the hospital for the past three hours, Ngosi's face was still a shock, yet he knew he had to stomach it.

Ngosi did not know much Portuguese, but he knew enough to sense that Kane was a foreigner. "Let's go!" Ngosi said, taking Kane's hand without hesitation. Kane looked at Ngosi with a soft smile, allowing the mini adventure to persist; it might be just the invite needed to break up his wild edginess. Ngosi's playful walk quickly turned into a sudden sprint. Releasing Kane's grip, he made for the abandoned white 1969 Ford Tora in front of them.

Ngosi, with his bare feet, climbed swiftly up to the top of the car. Suddenly, he soared high in the air, launching himself off the edge of the hood, rotating into a back somersault. It was flawless. Impossible. The only time Kane had seen anything like that was back home, in Brooklyn. He could not help but think of his own childhood. Ngosi had a novel way of making people forget their troubles for the moment.

Ngosi's tumble seemed to have summoned a deeper revelation. For the first time, besides having the same skin color, Kane felt a strange connection with the orphan; a connection too deep for any of the foreign aid workers or doctors to have felt. It was a sense of identity, of being connected, of being black—of being African.

A simple tumble forced Kane to finally take notice of the people around him. He did—especially Ngosi.

Even though they were separated by language, Kane managed to maintain a dialogue with the youngster through strong hand gestures and a mixture of really bad Spanish. They played a quiet game of Follow the Leader. Ngosi picked up the Brooklyn-born game as quick as any rascal in the east Brooklyn projects.

<hr>

Meanwhile, back at the church, Kgosi and Kweku were planning their next moves.

"Kweku," the minister called out, now on a first-name basis with the both of them. Kweku regretted it every time he'd call them. Kweku was convinced the minister liked their names because they were not traditional Angolan names. He passed Kweku some nuts and a soda pop, prepared by one of the sisters of the church. Kweku remained reserved, still slightly suspicious of the minister's kindness. Kweku watched as Kgosi knocked around a ball of string with a few kids behind the church. They were locked into a serious game of soccer. Kgosi convinced Kweku to stick around town for a day or so before attempting to head home. Kgosi's request came with little protest—fighting through the thick forest was no picnic.

Kweku was still absorbing things, always thinking. This time, his thoughts were filled with the minister's daughter from last night; he could not stop thinking about her. He sat against the side of the church wall, watching Kgosi make a fool of himself. Kgosi was no match for the little ones. The ground was dusty and dry, as if it never rained there. It was amazing how quickly the sun could dry things out.

"Go, go, go!" The children yelled, trying to chase down Kgosi's assault to the goal.

He stopped and then launched it.

The ball went soaring pass the narrowly placed sticks and down the steep overhang.

He scored.

The roar of the crowd took Kweku out of his daydream. It was the first time in weeks that he had the opportunity to fantasize about sex. Usually it was about Akua, although after eyeing the minister's daughter in the nude, it made good for some fresh thoughts. Kweku stood up, shaking his head in a half smile. The cheers continued. Kweku was baffled by the extended celebration. *It's just a game,* he thought to himself.

"Where's Kgosi?" He wondered. His eyes searched through the lifted dust.

Suddenly, a loud blast went off.

It shook Kweku to the ground.

The field emptied in seconds.

Everyone quickly made for the church, holding their ears.

"Kgosi!" Kweku shouted. "Kgosi!" Kweku yelled as he lifted his weapon from the wall and ducked down in a fighting position. Unbeknownst to him, the way he fell into position undoubtedly confirmed that he was a soldier—and a good one.

The dust settled, and after several cries for Kgosi, Kweku was nearly hysterical. He tightened the grip on his gun and carelessly ran into the middle of the open field. He knew it made him an open target but he didn't care. Kgosi was all he had. And for the first time, his emotions were getting the best of him. A deep nervous pain tore through his stomach.

He called out again, but still, no reply.

His eyes began to water, as he continued to scan the area.

Nothing.

The soccer players watched anxiously through the window. Even the minister was in total fright, watching Kweku through the cracks of the front door.

"Kgosi?" Kweku murmured softly, walking towards the homemade goal posts. Still, nothing. There were no visible signs of a combatant.

*A sniper perhaps.*

He knocked over the wooden goal post with his gun, frustrated.

Then, finally.

A sound.

It came from down the small cliff.

"Kgosi!" Kweku yelled out as he stumbled to the edge of the over-hang. Small rocks rolled off the edge, as he looked down in disbelief.

Blood covered Kgosi from the chest down. Kweku took notice of where Kgosi's left leg used to be. It had been ripped to shreds by a landmine. He had seen worst when his commander was killed, but this was Kgosi, his cousin. His normally steady hands began to tremble.

Kgosi had just gone to collect the makeshift ball that had flown through the goal post. It could have happened to anyone. Children fell victim to landmines daily all across the country.

Kgosi continued to moan on the withered grass. The pain was un-bearable for him. Kweku's fist tightened as he stood to his feet, shaking off his nerves. He quickly tucked his feelings away and went back to the fast-thinking soldier that Kgosi had always been able to depend on. He jumped down the six-foot overhang, disregarding his safety. He landed a few feet from Kgosi and ripped his green army shirt clean from his chest before tying it around Kgosi's left thigh. It slowed the bleeding, but the wound was horrendous; Kgosi's thighbone was completely exposed and pieces of flesh hung from all sides. Kweku ignored all of it, including Kgosi's violent screams as he finished dressing the wound. He threw him over his back and made for the church.

---

Meanwhile, back at the hospital, Kane was still enjoying Ngosi's company.

It was the first time he'd completely forgotten the plane crash and all that had happened since. His second day in Africa was soon coming to a close as the sun began to tuck its self beneath the barren town. He was still anxious to return home, though hanging around Ngosi made him feel more courageous for some reason.

Watching Ngosi play, he soon realized that the kid's dedication to happiness and a lively spirit was not an act. It was real—as real as the hymns pouring from the Angolans in church earlier. Kane knew nothing of this war and very little about Africa. Thanks to the media and his lack of exposure, he only knew Africans to be hungry and poor people. In the past thirty-six hours, he started to realize so much more.

He did not bother to feel sorry for the boy; it was clear that Ngosi could handle himself—perhaps even better than Kane could. He looked up to Ngosi, and respected him more than he had ever any gangsters hanging around the street corners in east Brooklyn. Ngosi knew he could die any hour of any day, but he still kept himself in good spirits—even after his family had been killed.

Suddenly, in a flash.

Two shadows quickly approached them from behind the trees. Kane startled, moved closer to Ngosi and held out his hand. Reaching for Ngosi's hand had been an unconscious impulse, one that instantly touched the orphan. He took hold of Kane's five fingers, without hesitation. It was obvious that Ngosi had made a huge impact on Kane. A few hours ago, Kane may have reacted to the shadows differently. Instead, he stood his ground and pulled Ngosi behind him as the two shadows came into the light.

Two unarmed men, locals, ran hysterically towards the hospital–one of them slipping by the entranceway.

*Something is wrong*, Kane thought to himself. He slowly headed to the entrance with Ngosi, concerned.

"Doctor!" The man said, trying to collect some much-needed air. They ran ten miles from a nearby market place. It was Mr. Obowei; he helped out around the hospital on weekends. The news of Sabovio's attack had leaked out, and with no phones for miles, many people were forced to run on foot to tell the neighbors. The hospital only had access to long-range walkie-talkies to enable them to communicate with NATO forces in the area. There were no phones.

"We will be attacked tonight! The rebels are coming this way!" Mr. Obowei was still out of breath, barely getting the words out. Rebecca, the unofficial head nurse, quickly placed her hand on Mr. Obowei's left shoulder, trying to calm him down.

"We will be attacked now! Tonight, by the rebels!" Mr. Obowei repeated the news.

"Base ten, base ten, pickup, pickup. We have a code red. Pick up base ten," the NATO forces were just getting word to the hospital. Rebecca, the clinic nurse, confused, eventually headed for the radio in disbelief. Many of the doctors were in the middle of surgeries and were not about to drop what they were doing on account of Sabovio. They were, along with the many Angolan citizens, the true soldiers. The heroes who sacrificed not only their high-paying jobs, but their lives as well.

The doctor picked up the radio and listened to every word with special care. The evacuation protocol was well-understood. Ten to fifteen NATO soldiers would arrive to pick up the hospital staff in the next hour or so. The doctors could usually persuade the NATO soldiers to take a few patients with severe conditions but not many. They would then be transported to a safe zone, most likely Pretoria, South Africa. Tragically, the remaining patients and locals would be on their own from that point.

Night was swiftly approaching and the winds were picking up, signaling a good chance of a downpour. Kane and Ngosi entered the hospital slowly.

"Come, I need your help," Rebecca said to Kane as she headed for the supply room. Kane was still holding onto Ngosi's hand, but he released it quickly in pursuit of the near-hysterical nurse. It seemed obvious that he would not be left to the slaughter.

Rebecca and a few foreign aid workers frantically began packing. She told him, "We are coming under attack. We will be leaving." Rebecca was more worried about the patients than she was about herself. She began shoving medical supplies into plastic bags. She wanted to pack as much as possible for the patients who were going to be left behind. Rebecca was a seasoned nurse. She was born in Denmark but grew up in Sydney. Her family was fairly wealthy. She already survived humanitarian trips into Cambodia and Ethiopia. She'd seen her fair share of death. Kane took her direction as if he'd worked there for months, helping patients off their beds and out the front door. He had already grown numb to the horrific injuries hours ago.

Meanwhile, back in town.

Kweku softly placed Kgosi near the front of the church, his ears still ringing from the blast. The minister and several of the young players rushed to his aid. Even the minister's daughter emerged. Her freshly washed white dress and carefully styled ponytail went unnoticed. Kweku was only interested in Kgosi.

"The car!" The minister shouted, dashing for his 1978 Chevrolet. It had just enough gas to make it to the hospital. Kgosi's vitals were stable, but the blood he lost had sapped his energy. He was still vibrating— moaning from the pain.

Kweku's shirt was performing perfectly around Kgosi leg. It was fixed firmly around his thigh, tied with love. It successfully stopped the blood loss for the moment.

*Yes, they will come from all sides of the city; we can only hide now.*
The minister listened to the radio, as his scruffy old car finally kicked
over. He paused for a moment, trying to understand the broadcast
while heading over in Kweku's direction. Kgosi moaned as Kweku lifted
him from the ground and headed for the back door of the car.

A slight drizzle began to fall. The night had finally approached.
Beginning to understand bits and pieces of what was being announced
on the radio, the minister ordered his daughter, José, into the car too.
He slammed on the gas and swirled gravel out from under the tires,
heading straight for the hospital.

Forty miles east of the hospital.

"Come," said the general, leaning back on a raggedy plastic school
chair they had collected some months ago from a missionary school. He
was ordering his son over for a Pepsi. The war held many levels of
complexity. A ruthless general, Sabovio was still a loving father. He
kept his son close by during clashes so he could protect him. Before the
different Black Liberation Movements had divided, Sabovio had been
well-known for his fight for independence against the White-controlled
Portuguese government. He fought them well, battling the Portuguese
armies in the interior of the country for years. Yet now, he was only
known for killing his fellow Africans. He was not alone. As the war
progressed, many formerly kind and admirable people lost their way. It
brought out the worst in many people—especially him. He had
developed an unyielding will to kill, and it had built him a terrible and
murderous reputation.

The second in command entered the battered kitchen. They were
stationed at the old, infamous Alexander de Santos house. Alexander de
Santos had been a White Portuguese politician who had made a living
by cheating Africans out of fair work wages. Everyone found it satisfy-

ing to see his house in ruins, but it was equally tragic to see it sheltering Sabovio's army.

Sabovio stood up, rubbed his son's head, and headed for his jeep. There was no moon. The sky was black. The only light came from their jeeps. The rain intensified, causing them to drive slower than normal. The foot soldiers armed with AK-47s and big knives followed the jeeps carefully, as they fought through the heavy downpour. They knew the town and the area intimately. The rain would not deter them. They would arrive soon.

—

Back at the hospital.

The rain had become torrential and the drivers of the NATO jeeps had turned off their engines for the moment. They were parked in front of the entranceway, sending a quiet message to new, incoming patients about the hospital's closure. Many of the doctors were finishing their surgeries, and patients who were able to move were struggling into the forest. The hospital already began to look abandoned, as it did before the UN's humanitarian relief organization had arrived fifteen months ago. This small city had once been home to three hospitals, but tank fire had destroyed those years ago.

Kane was still being extremely helpful for someone who had a house full of maids in Los Angeles. He continued to pack the equipment and supplies into the NATO jeeps. He watched helplessly as women and children walked away from the hospital, IVs still attached to their arms. Children, who were recovering from gunshot wounds were barely able to walk- whimpered with each step. The rain slowed the evacuation. This hospital's location was well-known; the rebels would surely make it one of their first battlegrounds.

They continued preparing the patients in each room. Kane helped Rebecca every chance he could. He stomached every wound—some so hideous that the only way to keep from vomiting was by thinking of his father smiling across at him in the kitchen when he was five. He continued diligently. He did not know if his affection for these people were growing or if he was just happy to go home. Maybe Ngosi's courageous display of strength allowed him to realize his own. He did not have much time to ponder over it, but worked as if he'd been there for years.

Hospital staff decided that Ngosi would at least accompany them to the safe zone. They would not be allowed to take him to South Africa, but evacuating him would still be, at least for the moment, saving his life. Ngosi and Kane were instructed to pack the UN truck with medical supplies. Kane turned sharply at the loud tapping sound.

It was the minister's 1978 Chevrolet, on its last bit of gas. It appeared out of nowhere and came to a screeching halt alongside the NATO jeep. The soldiers took aim at the humble vehicle, until one of the soldiers recognized the car.

"It's okay! It's okay," the soldier said. The minister was well-known, even by some of the NATO soldiers. Still, he slowly exited the car with both hands in the air. After listening to the radio for the last forty minutes, it was clear that everyone was on high alert. He understood their reaction.

The soldiers lowered their weapons as the minister headed for the back of the car. The door flew open, as Kweku eyed the minister with concern. Kgosi had gotten weaker.

Two curious NATO soldiers approached the vehicle. Disturbed by all the blood, they ordered a stretcher over to the car. They still had an hour or so before they had to leave and, because it was the minister, they allowed Kgosi into the hospital.

Kane jumped down from the truck, taking interest in the commotion. He recognized Kweku right away as they made for the entrance. Kweku turned towards Kane and threw a cold stare at him, but for the first time, Kane looked back without flinching. After being immersed in blood and wounds that would have kept anyone up for days, Kane had finally developed some much needed ruggedness. He got a quick glimpse of Kgosi as some of his blood leaked off the edge of the stretcher. He flashed back to the memory of his father exiting the bedroom on the stretcher, and to the image of Keys lying in a puddle of blood.

His thoughts were racing.

Time seemed to freeze for a moment.

He stood in the pouring rain, staring out at the trees. Ngosi looked on, smart enough to leave Kane alone for the moment. It was an awakening of sorts for the unlucky American. Kgosi's situation made him start to question his own life and purpose.

"Please," begged the minister, as the hospital door swung open. Rebecca took them to the emergency room. No one had the courage to tell the minister that they were ready to leave. Doctor Chin, who just finished an amputee, directed the minister into his operating room. Doctor Chin was the best surgeon on staff and had become rather quick with amputee patients. Kgosi was in luck.

Thirty minutes passed.

The hospital was nearly vacant. Most of the staff and a few patients were already in the jeeps and ready to go. Kweku, the minister, and his daughter waited impatiently outside the door. The minister knew Kgosi's surgery was not life threatening. He'd seen landmine amputees many times. It was time he was most anxious about. Listening to the radio on the way over, he fully understood what was at stake—his life and the life of his precious daughter. The minister was a humble man; maybe he was too humble. He wondered if his kindness would be his demise this day. He thought of the sisters at the church and the children.

*Would they survive this?*

*God be with them, please.* The minister prayed in silence.

Kweku, paced back and forth, waiting impatiently for any news. Then it occurred to him that he'd left his rifle behind in the car. Since Kgosi's accident, Kweku's emotions had become less controlled. He had not been able to focus clearly, and for the first time, he seemed to show his real age. He ran out the door to collect his weapon.

Shorty thereafter, the minister was relieved as Rebecca and Doctor Chin swung the door open, looking satisfied.

"He lost a lot of blood. He needs rest." Doctor Chin was exercising the same level of concern for Kgosi, regardless of the pending rebel attack. Rest or not, they had to leave. They were clearly running out of time.

Then.

The first sounds of weapons were discharged from afar.

They had to leave.

The rebels had arrived and were close.

Everyone stood around, suspended in stock. The minister turned to Rebecca and asked, "What now?" She knew there was no room for all of them in the NATO convoy. She had exhausted all of her energy convincing the NATO commander that Kane was part of the staff and that they needed to bring Ngosi along as well.

Her eyes said everything.

Every person left behind, tore her up inside. She knew they would most likely be killed.

The front doors to the hospital flew open. The NATO senior officer stormed in. He was enraged that they had held up the departure for an amputee surgery. "We are leaving now!" He said and headed back to the jeeps. Rebecca was speechless. She pulled off the surgical apron and headed for Kgosi. Lifting him to his feet, the minister and Rebecca headed for the front door. The doctor and José followed behind. Rebecca hoped to just jam them in the jeep. Maybe with all the heavy rain and commotion, the commander would not notice a few extra.

Kweku collected his rifle from the back seat of the minister's car. He turned back and smiled when he saw Kgosi's silhouette, missing leg and all. A deep weight was lifted off his chest as he headed in Kgosi's direction.

Kane watched Kgosi from inside the armored jeep. He looked around and notice there was no space for all of them. Turning back towards the window, he looked on as the senior officer and a few soldiers approached Kgosi. "We are not taking any more locals. You know this Miss Fiennes," the commander was beside himself. Kane looked on, watching Rebecca plead with the NATO commander. Kweku had arrived and carefully placed his rifle behind him. The argument continued and the NATO senior officer grew more agitated as he waved his finger in her face.

"Look, you all can stay here if you want. We are leaving now!" He yelled and walked away. He told them that the minister and his daughter were allowed to tag along with Dr. Chin and Rebecca, but that was it. Kgosi and Kweku could not accompany them.

He was not impressed by Kgosi's condition. In fact, he had turned away children in worse condition. The jeeps were full, and could not safely hold another person. Kane watched in disbelief as Kweku was left holding his injured cousin by himself. The minister walked to the jeep with his head down in shame. He intended to ride in the jeep with his daughter, but he had come to care for the two of them, especially Kgosi. It was difficult to leave them alone, but his daughter was his first priority.

You didn't have to speak Portuguese, or be from Angola to understand what was happening. Kweku and Kgosi struggled back into the deep grassland. The minister would have offered his car, but he knew it was out of gas. It would have been foolish to suggest it. Kane continued to stare on in disbelief.

Rain began to pour down the side of the window.

The jeep's engine roared to life.

*We are just going to leave them?* Kane could not believe it.

It was too much for him. Kweku and Kgosi had saved him. He felt as helpless as he had in the bathroom of Dunkin Donuts on the night that Keys had died.

Not this time.

"Stop!" Kane yelled, shouting over the pounding rain drops on the roof of the jeep.

"Stop," he requested again; this time in a quiet whisper. He turned back towards Kweku and Kgosi. They stood in the distance watching the rest of the jeeps drive off.

"Let me out!" He shouted again. He knew that if he left the jeep, the odds of him making it home were next to none. But, he could not leave them.

The jeep stopped.

"If you leave, you'll die," the NATO soldier said. He wanted to make sure Kane understood the gravity of the situation. As the door opened, Kane paused and thought about his life.

—

*It was the dead of autumn. Leaves covered the asphalt behind the building. Dimitri anxiously kicked the leaves aside for Kane's spectacular hurdle. Weeks had passed, and all of Kane's friends had hurdled over this bench. Even Tileyah had cleared it. It was the only thing he truly came to fear. The thought of his legs crashing against the tip of the bench, and his frail, nine-year-old body plummeting to the cold, hard cement had held him back from jumping it for weeks. Dimitri had ultimately convinced him that he had a chance. "You can do it," Dimitri shouted, as Kane took off, sprinting towards the bench.*

*Seconds later, Kane's worst fears were realized when his back foot clipped the bench. His fully airborne body, violently struck the cement, leaving a sharp line of cuts across his arm and knees. Dimitri, deeply worried, rushed to his aid. The worst had happened. And, despite the brisk autumn wind, Dimitri pulled his shirt off and wrapped it around Kane's right knee. He sat there frozen as Kane cried out in pain.*

*It was the first time Kane had ever experienced brotherly love. It lay over him like a thick blanket. He could feel it protecting him.*

—

Reluctantly, Kane nodded to the NATO driver, grabbed Ngosi's hand as hard as he could and headed out. It was a grasp so tight Ngosi had to fight off the pain, but understood what it meant. Goodbye. But not just any farewell. It was the one Kgosi was looking for when Kane first left him back at the church.

It was real.

Kweku and Kgosi watched on, uncertain of what to make of it. The minister watched on in shock as Kane jogged over to them. The anxious minister's grasp tightened on the door handle, as he turned his eyes to his daughter, conflicted. Every piece of his soul wanted to leave the jeep too. Aside from being a minister, he was a police officer in Kenya once, and leaving someone behind went against his nature. However, the minister remained fixed to his seat as the jeep sped off to catch the others.

# Chapter Sixteen

F INALLY, THE RAIN HAD LET UP SOME, but the night was darker than usual. The dark clouds still covered the sky. They had been walking for two hours, trying to get back to the church. It was a good place to rest, and the only place Kweku knew in the area. They walked parallel to the dirt road the minister had taken to the hospital, but they were careful not to be seen by passing cars on the road. The high grass kept them well-hidden. Since the NATO soldiers left them at the hospital, the sound of gunfire went off every few minutes. It was difficult to tell where the rebels were because the shots were coming from all directions. Kweku could just imagine the devastation.

They continued without resting and, to Kweku's surprise, Kane showed no signs of stopping. Perhaps the constant gunfire accounted for his steadiness. Clearly, he was unaccustomed to them. He flinched at every shot. Kweku, on the other hand, knew the sounds very well. In fact, it kept him focused. With Kgosi on his left arm and his AK-47 in his right, he was prepared to shoot on sight. At this point, he would shoot anything that moved. He just hoped some innocent little girl did not stumble too quickly onto their path. The small fragile town was now a killing field. And the three of them were at the center of it.

Kgosi was still very weak, and although Dr. Chin had done a great job with the surgery, pain from the stitches began to set in. Kgosi held it all in, keeping the moans to himself. He knew it would just be a distraction to the others. Besides, he was very happy to have Kane lifting him from the left side. To him they could travel several more miles without complaint.

Kweku was still puzzled by Kane's return, and so was Kgosi. However, with gunshots going off every ten seconds, they did not have a lot of time to ponder over it. He seemed more like help than a liability, unlike before.

With their clothes soaked from the rain, the return to the church seemed endless. Each stride was laboring and Kgosi was getting weaker. Kane had no idea where they were headed, but he felt Kweku's stride was confident enough not to make a fuss.

Suddenly, a light appeared in the distance. At first, Kweku thought it was from a light pole, but it was getting closer. He knew then that he was seeing the headlights of a car. Taking no chances, they quickly ducked beneath the high grass to avoid being seen.

The car edged closer.

Kweku noticed Kane's worried face and immediately placed his hand on Kane's shoulder. He tried to console the jittery American. An odd change of events; considering that twenty-four hours ago, he would have been disgusted at his reaction. So much had changed in the past twenty-four hours. Kane, although not regretting his decision to leave the jeep, could not help his edgy nature. The touch of Kweku's rugged hand gave Kane some comfort for the moment.

They heard tires slowly rubbing against gravel. The jeep pulled up right next to them. They made a wise decision to duck into the grass. The vehicle was populated with twelve armed rebels heading for the hospital, looking for trouble. Kweku, sensing the jeep slowing, quietly readied his rifle to his chest—preparing for a gunfight.

The jeep came to a full stop.

Kweku gasped.

He wrapped his finger around the trigger, as the voices moved closer. Kane snapped his eyes shut and began his desperate prayer to God.

*Did they see us? We are sitting ducks,* Kweku pondered, as his palms began to sweat.

Footsteps edged closer.

The headlights from the jeep covered much of the open field, but the bottom of the grass remained black and eerie.

One of the rebels seemed to notice something dark.

He moved in closer.

Suddenly, the sound of urine splashed against the wet soil, a few feet away from Kane's head. The rebel soldier noticed a small tree stump and decided to relieve himself there. They went unnoticed for the moment. Kane covered his nose from the smell. Kweku was relieved to now know that they had just stopped to urinate, but held his finger on the trigger of his riffle.

Moments later, the leader yelled, "Let's go!" As the footsteps began to trail away, Kane sighed in relief. At this point, he was sure God was protecting him.

As the jeeps sped off, Kweku made it clear that they should not get up too quickly. After ten minutes, they stood up and continued northward, hoping the church was nearby.

Three long hours later.

"Look," Kgosi said, surprised to be the first to take notice of the church off in the distance. He was in need of rest. The pain from the operation began to wear on him. Fresh blood stained the back of his worn out denims. Three stitches had re-opened during the vigorous five-hour journey. He knew he was bleeding but remained quiet. He thought: *What could they do about it anyway?* He just needed to be patient.

Moments later, they arrived to what was left of the church. The rebels had turned the already desolate place inside out. Although bodies were not in plain sight, a fresh stench of death filled the air. It was difficult to believe that this place had been filled with happy people singing and playing soccer, less than ten hours ago.

They surveyed the area, looking for a place to get water and, if they were lucky, something to eat. The plan was to head in the direction of the forest—back the way they came. The forest was the key to getting back to their village. Home.

"Wait here," Kweku said, softly placing Kgosi against a wall behind the steps of the church. He was out of plain sight—a good place to rest. With gestures, Kweku ordered Kane to watch over Kgosi until he returned. *Okay,* Kane nodded. He sat down calmly next to Kgosi and was careful not to hit his wound.

Kane's growing affection towards the both of them was unthinkable. He had no idea what their next step would be. He stepped out on faith and he believed in Kweku.

Kane watched as the oversized soldier lowered his back and walked, vigilantly away from the church with his rifle ready. Kweku could make anyone feel safe.

Kweku searched carefully for anything useful. He knew the forest would be laboring, especially with Kane in tow and Kgosi now injured.

Kgosi's moans got louder.

As Kane leaned his back against the wall, he tried to inquire about Kgosi's health. He wanted to know if the battered teen was okay. He was not. Kgosi felt the warmth of blood traveling down his backside. He saw the worry on Kane's face, but had no energy to try and explain things to him.

*I'll tell Kweku when he returns,* Kgosi thought to himself. It did not make sense to alarm Kane. The last thing Kgosi wanted was Kane running out there looking for Kweku alone. He gave Kane a slightly believable nod, reassuring him for the moment. Looking out at the open field where he had collected his thrilling goal, Kgosi grimaced. He hoped the children he played with earlier had managed to escape.

Although the rain had stopped for the moment, the wind was still strong and steady, indicating more rain to come. With no electricity now, the battered streets were lined in endless darkness. However, Kweku had grown used to it. He cautiously sauntered down the street, slithering behind collapsed buildings, looking for anything useful. He remembered that the petrol station had running water, although in this darkness, finding it would be a challenge.

Thirty minutes passed.

He could not find anything useful. He began to worry about the others.

*Maybe I'll find something on the way back to them,* he thought to himself. Kweku, feeling like a failure, turned back. He was growing tired of hiding and running. After a while, even a durable person like Kweku can show signs of breaking. He was only nineteen.

He started making his way back, thirsty and drained. Then suddenly, two shots echoed from nearby.

Kweku quickly dropped against the wall and pulled out his clip to inspect his rounds. He reconnected the clip and gripped his AK-47, listening for more sounds. He heard shuffling rocks and voices getting closer. Quickly, he turned and ran down towards a storefront. It looked like an old shoe store from the outside. As he looked around, he could tell that it had been an old shoe store, but now was refashioned into a bar. Shadows of liquor bottles lined the back wall.

The voices came closer.

Kweku swiftly made his way behind the counter top, trying to bury himself beneath the sheet-metal counter.

He paused suddenly, then gasped as he stumbled across two dead bodies—a man and a woman. They were both missing their arms and legs. They had only been dead a few hours. He had seen his share of dead bodies, but never quite got use to the sight of them. He grimaced and quickly realized the two slumbering corpses were occupying his hiding spot. He needed to move them quickly. The voices seemed to be headed directly into the bar. There was no time to be careful with the bodies. He grabbed the dead man and rolled him out of the way.

Shit! Kweku gasped.

He bumped into the back wall, causing a bottle of rum to tumble off the shelf.

It struck the ground, spilling in all directions.

"Did you hear that?" One rebel named Bakonga asked, as the other two rebels stopped in mid-stride. This part of town had been cleared nearly five hours ago, but they had been ordered to go back and collect anything of value—young women and liquor topped the list.

"This way!" Bakonga instructed. They lifted their rifles and headed straight for the bar.

Kweku heard their footsteps when they entered the bar. He did not have time to move the other body. If they peeked over the bar counter, they were sure to see him. Sighing at his predicament, he lay flat on the floor with his gun pointing up. He wanted to be able to shoot the first one to lean his head over the counter.

"Liquor!" Bakonga said, excited about the find—forgetting the noise.

"Go get it," the anxious leader said, pushing one of his soldiers towards the bar.

The soldier worked his way on top of the metal counter.

Kweku hardened his grip on his rifle.

He clutched his trigger finger.

Sweat poured from his face.

Danger was imminent.

The rebel reached the edge.

He exposed the front portion of his body over the counter in Kweku's plain sight, as he reached for the bottles.

Their eyes met quietly.

A quiet pause covered the moment. It seemed endless.

The rebel, his name was Mauiala. He was a sixteen-year-old that Bakonga had taken from his town when he was twelve. He had been a good kid once. Talented. He wanted to be a musician like his father. Before the war devastated his town, he was known around town as *Kwgoda*—little drummer boy.

Then, it happened.

Two bullets sliced through the right side of his head, killing him instantly. His body collapsed directly on the metal counter, allowing Kweku to reposition himself for the gunfight that was certain to follow.

Expectedly, a hail of gunfire tore the makeshift bar into pieces. Bakonga and the other soldier kept firing as they headed outside for cover.

Kweku only discharged a few rounds, conscious of his dwindling ammunition.

More shots hit the bar.

Some struck Mauiala's ribs and left calf.

His corpse was now part of Kweku's cover.

Meanwhile, back at the church.

Kgosi and Kane felt anxious when they heard the gunfire. It was less than a half mile away. Kgosi began to worry for his older cousin. They had never been out of each other's sight since they left the village.

Kane stood up, anxious.

"No!" Kgosi said, pulling Kane back to the ground. Kane flopped back against the wall, restless, praying that Kweku would show his face soon.

More shots.

Thunderous this time.

Bakonga was giving Kweku all he could handle.

Scorched gunfire sliced across more liquor bottles, clearing the last of them from the shelf. More cut into Mauiala's already tattered body. Kweku tried not to look at him. The rebels' gunfire continued striking the dead body, leaving behind a gruesome site.

Kweku returned fire.

*This is not working,* Kweku thought.

*I can't see anything. I'm shooting at nothing, wasting bullets and time.*

He knew more rebels would be on their way soon. Then he'd be truly outnumbered. He strained his eyes, looking for another way out.

*A door!* He sighed with relief. He didn't noticed Mauiala's fully loaded rifle, until now. He cleared it from his back and quickly headed for the back door.

More shots came at him from outside the ragged storefront.

"Go, we need more bullets! Call this in from the jeep," Bakonga ordered the other rebel soldier as he stood behind an overturned van. When the others received the call, it would be catastrophic. There were over three hundred rebel forces in the immediate area, and more on the way. Kweku had to get back to the others quickly.

Kweku was in luck. The side door opened without a hitch. He quietly crept inside and looked around.

"Ah," he said, relieved.

A window, but it seemed too small for him to fit through.

He jumped up to the elevated window and sized it up. After his quick survey he felt a bit more confident that he could make the squeeze. He threw the two guns out of the window first and then prayed that his oversized body would make it through. It meant that he would be unarmed for a moment. If he couldn't fit, he would have undoubtedly sealed his fate. Bakonga and the rest of the rebels would surely make quick work of him, especially with him dangling from the window unarmed.

He turned his head up in a quick grimace, hoping his decision was the right one. He scaled up to the window, focused. He felt uneasy without his weapons. He strained through the window and immediately regretted it.

He was wedged in.

He pulled harder.

Nothing.

He was a sitting duck. He closed his eyes and thought of home.

—

*It was a sunny day back home in the village. Kweku and Akua were younger. She was ten years old, and Kweku was turning twelve in a few* weeks. They had been told to go look for any Sbaba bean plants that grew outside the planting ground. It was a rare find, but she knew the plant well. It was the key ingredient in the beer for the upcoming festivities.

"Let's go," Akua said, pointing out into the forest. She was always the one suggesting the unexpected, and Kweku never let her down. The forest was forbidden for children. Leopards, wild boars, and many other wild animals were never far away.

As they entered, a slight mist began to hover over the towering treetops, instantly bringing with it a dim eeriness to a rather sunny day. Akua lived for these moments. She loved a thrill more than the other ten-year olds.

They had been walking for fifteen minutes.

"Akua, let's go back," Kweku said, not bothered by the darkness but worried for Akua's safety. With no weapon to protect her or himself, he thought it was not wise to go any further.

Suddenly, a deep growl struck their ears.

It was an animal.

Akua threw herself behind Kweku, clutching his waist for dear life. It was the first time Kweku felt like a man. It was the first time he had to protect someone. Although constantly hunting with his brothers and uncles, he had never been left alone to fend for himself. His heart was pounding vigorously. He hoped Akua did not sense his anxiety. Still remembering not to run at the first sign of a threat, he fixed himself there and surveyed the area for a weapon.

A rock.

He spotted it just a few feet from him. It was large enough to cause damage if he threw it carefully. He picked it up and backed away slowly, looking in all directions for the source of the noise.

The growls grew louder.

Akua's hands started to tremble.

"Look Kweku! Look!" Akua said and pointed towards the tree.

*It was a leopard.*

*It stood there staring into Kweku's eyes.*

*Kweku kept still—frozen. His eyes did not release its hold on the beast. He kept Akua behind him and stood there with a steadiness that impressed the adventurous ten-year old. She had only seen her uncles carry that type of confidence. The leopard growled again and inched closer. Kweku stood there clutching his rock. Sweat poured from his face.*

*Suddenly, the leopard pounced. Kweku closed his eyes and flung the rock at the beast. When they opened, the leopard was dead. For a moment he thought he killed it, but soon noticed the oversized arrow lodged in the side of its' head.*

*"Akua," a man's voice shouted from behind. It was Akua's uncle, Babeioka. He walked up behind them with a serious look on his face. He was unbelievably relaxed. He had been impressed by Kweku. He watched the entire episode unfold. He knelt down next to the fallen creature. "This is your kill, Kweku."*

*Akua and Kweku unconsciously held hands the entire walk home, listening to hunting tales from Babeioka. He was always one of the energetic storytellers.*

*Since then Kweku had grown into a bold and fearless man. His unwavering strength was needed once more.*

Back in the bathroom window.

Kweku's eyes widened as he gripped the edge of the window with all his might. In his last attempt to pull himself through, he initiated a violent tuck maneuver that managed to propel his arms through the hole. Only his waist and legs remained in the bathroom. Ignoring the pain of peeled skin being stripped by the rigged cement corners, he continued fighting his way through the God-forsaken hole.

Finally, his body flopped down two feet from his weapons.

He sprung to his feet, swiped the guns from the grass, and headed straight for Kgosi and Kane.

The wind had picked up again. He watched the trees out near the forest lean to the side. Rain was near, making travel worse for them. Kweku took off in a full sprint. At this point, he did not care if someone spotted him. They needed to get to the forest quickly. Soon the area would be crawling with rebels.

Moments later.

"Kgosi!" He yelled, as he turned the corner to the church. They were still alive, but Kgosi's condition had worsened. Kweku finally took notice. Their eyes met and Kweku detected the grim truth. He'd seen that look in Kirabo's eyes a few weeks ago just before he had died.

"Let's go!" Kweku handed over Mauiala's bloodstained rifle to Kane. He did not bother to tell them that they were in danger or how to use it. Kane collected the rifle, following Kweku's lead.

They had no choice but to head through the open field where the soccer game had been played earlier. It was the fastest way back to the forest. They started their trek through the open field. Suddenly, an oversized raindrop caught the left side of Kgosi's neck, then another. The rain had arrived again, more demanding than earlier. It slowed their stride, forcing them to arch their backs. It was unbearable. Kweku knew it would not last for long and made it clear that they would not be stopping as his pace quickened.

Suddenly, a loud blast came from the church.

It was Bakonga.

He fired a few rounds through the rain. He tracked Kweku from the bar. He had been fixed on their location the entire time.

He looked up through the thick rain, searching for a good shot.

He fired again.

The bullets missed Kane's head by mere inches. They all fell to the ground and began to crawl.

"Shit!" Kane yelled. He pulled the rifle from his back. They were in a difficult position to return fire. The best thing they could do now was to keep moving forward.

Bakonga continued to peer through the rain in search of their shadows.

"Where did they go?" Bakonga asked himself, puzzled. The rain had certainly saved them for the moment. It was difficult seeing anything through it.

Bakonga fired more shots in frustration.

They finally reached the edge where the overhang was located. Kgosi remembered this spot vividly. It was the same location where he lost his leg.

A possible minefield—a death trap.

Kweku sighed.

They had no choice. They started exactly where Kgosi lost his leg. It took all of five seconds for Kane to understand Kgosi's description of the mine field. He simply pointed to his leg and then to the ground. Kane tightened up his crawl. With every forward motion, they all knew their life could end. They pressed on with their hands sinking down in the thick mud. Suddenly, Kane hesitated. He spotted partially exposed metal-inches away from his right hand. He was certain it was a mine, slightly exposed by the heavy rain. It didn't make sense to warn the others, as he was last in line. He just kept moving, numb, knowing his life could end at any moment.

Within minutes, a few of Bakonga's men arrived at the church. There were now six of them, with more on the way. They were headed straight for the minefield.

Boots splashed against saturated soil.

Dark water ran off the edges of their machetes.

They were moments away from the overhang.

Kweku continued his careful crawl through the field, finding it hard to believe they were still in one piece. They had already traveled fifty feet away from the edge of the minefield. With nearly a hundred yards until they reached the forest, Kweku had to make a choice soon. He sensed that Bakonga would soon reach the overhang and would have a clear shot at them.

Kgosi's bandage was nearly torn off from the brisk scramble. Three more stitches came loose. Kane could see the blood seeping from the wound, but could do nothing for him at this point. They needed to clear the minefield first. He turned his eyes back to the ground staying wary of each movement forward.

Bakonga and a few others reached the overhang.

He spotted them in plain sight and took aim.

Bakonga fired first.

His bullet sliced through Kweku's left leg. His left calf burned from the bullet wound. The mine field was now an afterthought as Kweku rolled over to return fire.

Kane rolled over and returned fire with Kweku. The kickback nearly took the riffle right out of Kane's hand.

He collected himself and fired again. His second round of shots tore through Bakonga's chest, killing him instantly. His lucky shot sent the other rebels to the ground. Kweku quickly rose to his feet, rushing to collect Kgosi. They could not crawl any longer. They stood up in a sprint to the forest. Being careful of the minefield was no longer their concern. They needed cover or they were dead anyway.

The rebels looked at Bakonga's body, stood up and began firing nonstop. They hit Kweku across his left arm and grazed Kgosi across his right side, as if the battered African needed another injury.

Kgosi moaned, feeling the pain from the bullet. They stumbled behind a tree at the edge of the forest. Kweku was relived, even with two bullet wounds. Kweku and Kane stood up and fired a few rounds from behind the tree. Kweku turned towards Kane, surprised. Kweku could not help but notice the conviction and poise in Kane's face. He smiled quietly and turned back to the fight.

The rebels slithered down the overhang to get closer. Within minutes, a deafening blast was heard. A mine had cleanly removed the bottom half of one of the rebels.

Another blast went off.

Then another.

What was left of Bakonga's men safely returned to the back wall. At this point, they were more concerned with retreating from the minefield than with shooting at Kweku and Kane.

The sound of war halted for a moment, as all of Bakonga's men tried to regain safe ground.

The rain dissipated, as Kweku and his battered bunch headed deeper into the forest.

The bullets had only grazed them, taking off a modest piece of skin. Kweku tightly wrapped his injury, while he watched Kane remove his shirt to redress Kgosi's left leg. With every moment that passed, Kweku's respect for Kane grew. He had forgotten that Kane was an

American and had only been in the country for less than two days. He knew now that he'd protect Kane with his life if necessary. Kane was family now.

# Chapter Seventeen

"AH!" KGOSI GASPED louder. His deteriorating condition fully grabbed Kweku's attention. They'd been fighting through the dense forest for a few hours now. With no sign of the rebels, it was time to rest. They all collapsed against the side of a fallen tree; safely out of plain sight. Kane was too tired to care about the noises of the forest anymore. Like Kweku, he simply placed his rifle against his chest and prepared for a light sleep.

Meanwhile, back at the church.

Nearly five hundred rebel forces assembled to set up a base camp in front of the church. The skirmish had gotten the attention of half the rebel force summoned to that area. They thought the northern army was in the area and began preparing for a gunfight. They were less concerned about chasing down a few soldiers. Their main goal was to control the area as long as they could until the South African army arrived with tank fire.

Several hours had passed.

The forest was still misty and damp from the night before. It was nearly noon. They'd been asleep for hours. Luckily, the wildlife had left them alone. Kweku was the first to awake to the bad news.

His heart tore into pieces when he looked over at Kgosi's face.

It was stiff.

His skin was frozen.

He was dead.

The would-be king had bled out during the night with his eyes still open. Falling back against the tree, Kweku tried desperately not to weep, but tears stumbled from his eyes as he moved over to shut Kgosi's eyelids. They were the first tears Kweku had shed since he was a child. He had never shown much emotion. He flopped against the tree base to collect himself before Kane awakened.

The war had taken his two younger cousins. Kgosi, a believer of all the old tales and strict follower of the village's traditions, would have made a good king. Kweku had always secretly admired him. He stood up, and quickly struggled to remove the tears from his face as Kane's eyes began to open.

Startled by Kgosi's stiff arm lying across his own, Kane jumped up and took a quick look over at Kweku. His face told the story, as Kane slowly backed away from Kgosi's body, deflated.

They found some sizable sticks and began digging a grave. Kane did not complain once about his thirst or hunger. He knew now what he did not before—this is no place for complaints or tears.

It took them a few hours, but they managed to bury Kgosi. It was more than Kweku had been able to do for Kirabo. They departed—exhausted yet relieved that they had accomplished the grueling task, without water. Kweku felt satisfied that he had the opportunity to bury Kgosi. In his village, it was important to do so. The elders claimed that when a body was left unburied the soul was not at rest.

It was time to move on. The night would come soon, making their search for food more difficult. Kweku took one lasting stare at Kgosi's grave then disappeared into the dense part of the forest with Kane.

# Chapter Eighteen

E IGHT DAYS HAD PASSED, and they were deep in the heart of the forest. Kweku could pick up the cold air and faint smells of fresh water. He knew the mountains were close. They were almost home. Kane had never tried to ask Kweku about where they were headed. Kweku always traveled as if he knew where he was going. Kane always assumed they were going to another town with more doctors and NATO soldiers like the one he had come across in the other town.

The eight days were easy. Kweku had killed a wild pig, dug a hole to cook it, and collected fresh water from the rain. They ate well on their journey. And, though Kweku was younger, Kane looked up to him as if the overgrown nineteen-year old was his older brother.

Even the mosquitoes kept away from him; more so now since the air was becoming cooler. Two days ago, they had talked more and learned each other's names. Kweku had even taught Kane some useful Kimbundu words. He did not bother with Portuguese. They were headed to the village where Portuguese was rarely spoken. Kweku became more at peace with each step because he knew the village was nearby. He could not conceal his jovial behavior from Kane. He was more talkative now than he had ever been. Kane watched his transformation unfold. It was strange to watch Kweku finally act his age, but it gave Kane a deep sense of comfort.

"Look!" Kweku shouted, pointing out a mango tree. He knew they were close. His blood began to pump with anxiety. They sprinted for the tree.

Kweku shook the branches and brought down five freshly ripe mangoes.

They all looked delicious.

Kane collected them immediately.

"My home is near," Kweku said, grasping Kane by the shoulders. His eyes were filled with contentment—hands full with fresh mangoes. It was the perfect treat after all they'd been through.

Their thirsty teeth crushed against the cool, fresh, mouth-watering fruit. Juices from the mangoes splashed across the bottom part of their mouths with every bite. They quietly devoured as many as they could. After nearly an hour, they decided to take some for the road. Kweku climbed high in the tree and tossed them inside the webbing Kane made with his shirt.

Kweku jumped down after the tenth one. Kane was thoroughly impressed by Kweku's hurl down the thirty-foot drop.

"Okay, let's go," Kweku said, taking the mangoes from Kane.

One fell to the ground.

Kane bent down to pick it up.

Then.

A blast slashed through the forest, like a knife.

It shook the mangoes loose from Kweku's hold.

A gunshot.

It rang out from nearby. It was the loudest one Kweku had ever heard since he joined the war. With his heart nearly coming to a stop, he collapsed to the ground in utter shock. He turned towards Kane and his face dropped in disbelief.

Kane's chest was covered in blood. The bullet had cut right through his upper body. He fell to his knees in utter shock. He tried desperately to reach for his rifle.

But he couldn't.

Then more bullets went flying.

They tore a hole through Kane's side. Kweku quickly collected his rifle and returned fire. With one arm he grabbed Kane by the arm, dragging him behind the tree.

More shots rang out.

Kane was still alive—but barely. The immediate shock had left. What was left now were Kweku's eyes, they were blood red, filled with rage.

The shooting persisted.

A few more shots sliced into the mango tree. Kweku, in a fury, stepped out from behind the tree disregarding his life and started firing.

One of the men behind the tree attempted to return fire.

No such luck.

Kweku's bullet pierced through the middle of the soldier's neck.

Another soldier stepped out.

Kweku hit him square in the face. He died instantly.

Kweku was so enraged; he did not realize he had run out of bullets.

Suddenly, another man sprung from behind the tree.

Amandio!

They had been searching for them in the forest for nearly two weeks. Kweku and Kane were eating from the very tree that Amandio and his men had slept under for the past few days. They were headed back to their base camp tomorrow. It was their luck to run into Kweku and Kane today.

Kweku's eyes widened.

Amandio paused, taking in Kweku's shock at seeing his face.

Kweku pulled the trigger.

Nothing.

A devilish grin crossed Amandio's face. He wanted to kill Kweku for the longest time.

He lifted his weapon.

Then.

A gunshot exploded from behind Kweku.

It was from Kane.

His bullet struck Amandio in the forehead, killing him instantly. Amandio fell forward and crashed to the ground. Kweku turned around astonished. He saw a barely-alive Kane struggling to hold up his rifle while he leaned against the side of the tree. Kweku dashed back over as Kane slid down the tree, practically limp.

Kweku quickly looked around for any of Amandio's men, but saw that they had killed them all. The fresh smell of gun smoke stained the air, reminding Kweku of all that had happened over the past year.

He held Kane's hand and watched on as his adopted brother struggled for life.

His breaths became softer.

And softer.

Looking around—fighting back tears, Kweku's grip tightened around Kane's hand, revealing all that words could not say.

Kweku took a deep sigh, then peaceful bent down and placed his hands affectionately on Kane's left cheek.

"It's okay. It's okay, brother," Kweku said in a soft whisper. He knew Kane was dying.

But it was a great death.

Within seconds, Kane's traumatized face calmed into a cool stillness. He clutched Kweku's hand one last time and then dropped back lifelessly against the tree.

He was gone.

Kweku slid down the tree and tried to come to grips with everything: the fighting, his cousins' deaths, and now Kane's. An American who decided not to abandon him and, in the end, saved his life.

It was a display of brotherhood and sacrifice so extraordinary that it could only be told as a folktale. No one would believe it.

Kweku buried Kane without tears, but with a smile. The voices of elders spilled back into his empty heart, drained by the war. Kane made him believe in love again. Not long afterwards, he also buried Amandio and his men. It was something Kgosi would have done.

Kweku finally understood pure hatred, peace, and now love. He prayed over the bodies and disappeared into the dark of the forest.

—

One year later.

"Come, come," Kweku said, standing out in the forest and signaling Akua over. An entire season had passed, and although the war continued, Kweku was safe once again, behind the secrecy of his village.

The trees began to sway.

Kweku clutched Akua's right hand.

He wanted to take in the first winds before the rainy season. He waited patiently for Kane's spirit to drift pass his face.

# The Incidents of War

"**G**ET OVER HERE!" Sabovio commanded one of his soldiers. Over the past year, his rebel force became a legitimate army. After the incident with Kweku and Kane, they became more aggressive. No longer did they settle for easy targets and light conflicts. They broke off their partnership with the South African army and recruited every one they could find—including women. It was: fight with them or be killed. The people were not given much choice. The result: Sabovio had the largest number of foot soldiers of the four armies. They were ready to take a large city; the South African-controlled Benguela was first, then northward to Luanda. Sabovio knew Benguela well. Aside from being born there, his soldiers helped the South African army gain control of it from the Northern Army. He had intimate knowledge of many South African positions and had the support of the locals as well.

A soldier dashed over and fixed herself in front of him. She could not have been more than ten. "Go wait in the jeep with Nodji," said Sabovio in a forceful voice. She reminded him of his first child. His daughter. She was raped and killed by a drunken soldier from the Northern Army.

Sabovio was a well-known butcher in northern Benguela. People knew him as a funny man, who would always poke light fun at some of the white people that frequent his shop. However, since the death of his daughter Awaji, he was a changed man. Her death filled him with rage.

Eventually, he found the soldier that raped and killed her. He slaughtered the man, but he was not satisfied. He wanted to kill them all, but over the years it became difficult to determine who the enemy was. He made it simple. Anyone not from Benguela could be the enemy, and anyone he thought was supporting the Northern Army was slaughtered.

Many had died because of him; mostly the innocent. Although now, his goal was different. "Free Angola," that was the message. He realized after years of consorting with the South Africans and interrogating commanders from the Northern Army, that the war was about a scramble for the country's resources—nothing more. He was no longer handcuffed by his rage from the death of his daughter. His decisions were calculating. They contained no emotions, except this one, to send the little girl to the jeep with his son. He did not want her in harm's way. Their mission was to take the western part of Benguela from the South Africans. It was a bold move. It was their central headquarters. If Sabovio succeeded, it would weaken the South African's entire position in the war.

"General," one of Sabovio's top commanders' voices came over the radio. Although Sabovio was in command of the entire UNDA force, he liked to be called general. It clearly defined his position as a hands-on leader. He was near the front line during every meaningful gunfight, and his men respected him for that.

"Go," Sabovio instructed, as he watched the ten-year old shut the jeep door behind her. She was safe.

"We are ready," said the commander in a strict and certain voice. *It will be a nasty fight,* Sabovio thought to himself. He paused and thought of the causalities, and then gave the order.

"Okay, go!"

⸺

Two months later, back in Kweku's village.

"Kweku. Help," Akua commanded him to help her off the ground. They had just finished listening to one of Gdobije's folktales. Gdobije was the oldest elder of the village.

Kweku helped her to her feet and smirked proudly at her oversized belly. She was pregnant and expecting any day now. Kweku, as expected, was extremely helpful and followed Akua's every command.

"Listen, Kweku you must find the Bali flower. It is bad luck to have a child without it," Akua said in a worried voice.

"Yes, I know. I will look tonight," Kweku said.

"No, not tonight," Akua said as she smiled into his eyes. She pulled him closer. He smiled lightly as her belly blocked her full hug.

"Okay, lets go, but no…" he instructed as he grabbed her hand. Ever since Kweku had returned home, Akua had developed a healthy addiction to the forbidden waterfall. They made love there countless times.

"Yes, of course," Akua replied sarcastically, knowing that as much as he would try to restrain from making love to her in fear of hurting their child, in the end; she would get her way.

⸺

Back at Sabovio's central command post.

"The first platoon should attack from Malange. The forest is thick there. It would be difficult for the choppers to see," Sabovio's lead commander explained. It was only six miles from their current location, and the first meaningful military post for the Northern Army.

Sabovio had successfully taken Benguela. And, as a result, the South African Army retreated to their auxiliary base in Namibia.

They had won. However, it came with a heavy price. Sabovio lost half his men. He was able to recruit some new soldiers inspired by the victory, but his army was greatly reduced. Sabovio did not want to wait to attack Luanda. He had fought in this war long enough to know momentum was everything. If the soldiers were to rest too long or not eat regularly, they would run away or be less inclined to fight with conviction. It had to happen now.

"Yes, Malange and Caxito, as well," Sabovio instructed. Caxito was a bigger base than Malange and it was said they had a wall of firepower there protecting the entire Northern Army's military supplies. However, trying to take it conventionally could be suicidal.

"They are too close together. If we do not attack them at the same time, they will fly and drop bombs on us," Sabovio explained. It was known that the base in Malange was a trap. If you tried to attack it, the base from Caxito would fly over and destroy your ground forces.

Sabovio went on to explain that they must attack Caxito first and weaken their flying capabilities, then fully attack Malange with most of the men.

"Okay, understood," the commander, answered. It was a death trap, splitting his army up this way, but he knew taking control of the base was the key to defeating the Northern Army.

They turned to each other and nodded their heads in agreement. One single nod said a million words. They knew they would never see each other again. They caught each other's eyes for a second. It was their way of saying goodbye.

"Come Nodji. You must go home with Obomi," Sabovio instructed his son.

"Home?" Nodji responded. "Yes, back to Benguela," Sabovio explained. He knew what he was up against and wanted his son as far away as possible. He kissed Nodji on the top of his head and put him in the jeep. The ten-year old girl, Mawou, followed behind. "Go," Sabovio shouted as he hit the top of the jeep. It spun off as the first drops of rain struck Sabovio across his forearm. *Yes, rain*, Sabovio thought to himself. It would be difficult for the airplanes and choppers to see them on the ground.

Sabovio led his half of the army to Malange. "Listen, tomorrow Angola will be free!" Sabovio shouted through the massive crowd of men.

A loud deafening roar vibrated through the forest. The men and women cheered.

"God is here tonight. We will take our country back from the thieves. Are you with me?" Sabovio shouted at the top of his lungs.

Loud cheers roared through the crowd.

The rain was now a downpour as Sabovio lead his soldiers to Malange.

---

Meanwhile, back at Kweku's village.

Kweku and Akua finally made it to the waterfall. It was raging from the rainfall. Kweku had grown uncomfortable bringing her there. There were too many rocks good for slipping on, especially in the rain.

"Come, Hunter," Akua called out while Kweku cleared some rocks from her path. "Stop with those rocks and stand up," Akua requested. A slight touch of the moonlight stole a peak through the thick clouds.

It was enough for Kweku to see the top of his hand. It was covered red with blood. He searched his hand frantically for a cut.

Nothing.

Then he looked over at Akua's feet. It was covered in blood. He followed the stream of blood up her leg and then realized she was bleeding.

"Akua you are bleeding," he said. She clutched her side and then took notice of the warm sensation running down her thigh. He swept her off the ground in one motion and headed back to the village.

"Kweku, we need the flower," Akua requested in a faint voice. Her eyes were blood red and closing slowly.

"Madouji Mama, Madouji Mama," Kweku's voice pierced through the village like a fresh blade.

"Give her to me," Madouji Mama ordered. Her swift voice gave Kweku some much-needed relief. He looked on as his aunts and the other elder woman crowed around her.

"Kweku," Madouji Mama shouted, "find the Bali!"

Kweku eyed her and then nodded his head quickly. He stood to his feet and ran towards the forest.

—

Meanwhile, back at Caxito.

The rain pummeled the ground like rocks. The commander had already gotten word from Sabovio to attack when he was ready. And, for the first time, after all his years of fighting for Sabovio, Knoidi felt he was part of something that had a true purpose. A great ball of energy rose to the top of his chest.

"Ready men!" Knoidi yelled with all the force he could gather.

"Go," Knoidi ordered his men.

The Northern Army was caught by surprise. Knoidi's unit killed a few soldiers that were outside the barricade. Their firepower could be heard for miles.

Then suddenly.

"Stop, stop!" Knoidi yelled after he took notice of the large cement wall with firing holes. It stared down at them like a big giant. The Wall of Fire everyone spoke of. He commanded all units to stop firing and take cover.

"What now?" Knoidi's key lieutenant questioned with a worried voice.

"Take the men to Unit Four, and leave me with thirty men wearing dark clothes."

The lieutenant followed his command without question. Knoidi was Sabovio's best general. He was behind most of Sabovio's military successes over the years.

Knoidi looked up and saw the first choppers hovering around the area. His goal was to breach the wall and take out some of their air capabilities. *We don't have much time*, he sighed to himself. The rain would help a bit, but not for long.

Moments later.

"General, we are ready," Knoidi's most trusted lieutenant stated. "Okay, fire when ready," Knoidi commanded.

The firing was immeasurable – crippling. They fired their weapons nonstop. They needed to cause a diversion for what Knoidi was about to do next.

Then came the return fire.

It was coming from the wall. It was massive, but so far, Knoidi's plan was working. The Northern Army started to put more attention on Unit Four. Knoidi got word from his lieutenant to proceed.

"Ready?" Knoidi asked his humble thirty-man team. They nodded yes. Next, they dropped down as low as they could and began a quick crawl to the wall. They had to hurry as they were in plain sight.

Suddenly, there was a loud explosion. Knoidi grabbed both ears. When the ringing stopped, he grimaced at the solider next to him. The man was in pieces after crawling over a landmine.

"Stop, stop," Knoidi yelled out, and instructed his men to get behind him. The men obeyed quickly, astonished at his bravery. He would be killed before any of them if there were other mines.

Finally, the soldiers arrived at the wall with no further incident. The wall was taller than Knoidi had expected and, with no rope, it was impossible to get over. "Give me your grenades," Knoidi ordered the soldier next to him.

"Give me your grenades. I need them all," Knoidi continued, ordering the rest of his men. He took his shirt off and collected them all. He put them in his shirt and kept one in his hand. He looked at the top of the wall and then at his makeshift bomb. If it lands just over the wall, it could blow a hole big enough for his men to crawl through. He only had one shot.

He tied his shirt around the grenades.

He put the last grenade in his mouth and pulled the pin out with his teeth.

He stuffed it in the shirt with the rest and threw it over the wall. They all ran for cover.

The grenades exploded.

Knoidi marched in quickly to investigate. There it was – a huge void. The bomb worked and the men were able to walk through, easily.

They breeched the wall, but the blast got the attention of some men in the area. They were fired upon immediately. Two of his men were killed instantly. Knoidi and the rest of his small unit took cover behind an empty tank, as the firing continued.

"Cover me!" Knoidi commanded. He headed inside the tank. It was armed and ready for use. Knoidi turned the tank to the enemies and fired. The blast was catastrophic. It killed nearly all the men in the area. Knoidi started to fire at will, taking out a fighter jet and two choppers. They pressed forward and were able to hit key targets, including two more choppers overhead.

Then, finally, the message came in from Knoidi—the one Sabovio was waiting desperately for: "We are over. Go," Knoidi gave Sabovio the cue to attack the base at Malange.

"Angolans, they have broken the walls at Caxito. My people, to-night Angola will be free," Sabovio shouted. But, it would not be freed. He was unaware that the South African army had joined forces with the Northern Army. They joined two days after Sabovio defeated them. Now, they were out-numbered three to one. The Malange base was crawling with South African soldiers and soldiers from the Northern Army. They were waiting for Sabovio. They knew he would attack there.

Sabovio, unaware of the situation, gave the command: "Fire!"

They did.

A hail of gunfire came from Sabovio's army.

And then the return fire from the Malange base. It all sounded as if the earth was splitting in two.

Sabovio looked up and saw several planes fly over his head. He looked at his men and watched in disbelief as twelve South African choppers fired down on his men, with more on the way. He started to realize the calamity of the situation. They were overwhelmed and outnumbered.

He took a deep breath and shouted, "Free Angola!" He turned back towards the enemy, stood up and started firing.

Seconds later, a hail of bullets struck his chest.

He was gone.

Not long after, his entire army had fallen. The South African army was surprised that none of Sabovio's men surrendered. They had all decided to fire until they were killed.

—

Meanwhile, back at Kweku's village.

Kweku ran as fast as he could, despite hearing gunshots off in the distance.

*This plant is impossible to find,* Kweku thought to himself. He decided to go deeper into the forest.

Suddenly, he stopped and there it was.

It stood there in the middle of nowhere. *Amazing,* Kweku thought to himself.

He went over to pick it up.

Suddenly, he felt a sharp lash cross his face. He fell to the ground, dazed.

"On the ground, Kaffir," a South African soldier ordered. They were all over the forest.

"Kill him and lets go," the other soldier instructed.

"What's over here, Kaffir?" The soldier questioned Kweku. He took notice that Kweku was dressed in leopard's cloth with no shoes. It was clear Kweku was not a soldier.

"Answer me, Kaffir," the soldier yelled, agitated.

"He can't understand you mate," reasoned the other soldier. But he pushed his riffle against the back of Kweku's head, anyway. Kweku clutched the Bali flower in his hand and put Akua's face in his thoughts.

The soldier put his finger around the trigger.

"Wait. Listen. The war is over. We won," the soldier fired a few shots in the air. Kweku dropped the flower. He thought he was dead. The soldier pressed his rifle against Kweku's head and said, "It's your lucky day, Kaffir. Go!"

Kweku picked up the Bali flower and headed back to the village.

———

Moments later.

"Here you are Kweku. Hunter, my Hunter. Here is your son." Akua said in a soft voice as she handed over the newborn. She noticed the Bali flower in his hand and smiled.

# Special Thanks

I 'd LIKE TO FIRST THANK, GOD. I believe he has really given me the strength and patience to finish this book. I'd like to thank everyone that was involved with this book in one way or another, Latonya Walker for her support, encouragement and strong opinions. All my friends from Brasil, Angola and the U.S. that supported me and who would constantly inquire about the book. Thank you. I would like to thank all who edited the book out of its natural form, my wife Anastacia Prince-Walker thank you so much; I couldn't have finished the book without you, really. I love you. Charlene Drayton thanks so much for getting this whole editing process started. I would also like to thank Edit Queen, Inc. for laying out the foundation; I would have been in a bad place without your help. Thank you Kimberly Martin for the layout and design. Also, I would like to give a big "Thank You" to Narolyn Clase for designing the book cover and Russell Pope for making critical enhancements to the book cover. Thank you so much. I deeply appreciate it.

I recently lost my Grandmother, my rock. This book is dedicated to her. She supported me with an unyielding conviction. I simply loved her most for just loving me as a child. I was never short a kiss, ginger snap or Christmas present each year.

In addition, I just want to give a big hello to my three kids, Jahsan, Jordin and Christian. They really keep me going, giving me a deep sense of purpose. I will always live trying to protect and support the three of them throughout their lives. Lastly, I want to thank my mom and my entire family for their undying support.